Acting Edition

Tuck Everlasting

Book by
Claudia Shear & Tim Federle

Music by
Chris Miller

Lyrics by
Nathan Tysen

Based on the novel by
Natalie Babbitt

Orchestrations by
John Clancy

Vocal Arrangements by
Chris Miller

Dance Music Arranged by
David Chase

‖SAMUEL FRENCH‖

ISBN 978-0-573-70544-1

www.concordtheatricals.com
www.concordtheatricals.co.uk

FOR PRODUCTION INQUIRIES

UNITED STATES AND CANADA
info@concordtheatricals.com
1-866-979-0447

UNITED KINGDOM AND EUROPE
licensing@concordtheatricals.co.uk
020-7054-7298

Each title is subject to availability from Concord Theatricals Corp., depending upon country of performance. Please be aware that *TUCK EVERLASTING* may not be licensed by Concord Theatricals Corp. in your territory. Professional and amateur producers should contact the nearest Concord Theatricals Corp. office or licensing partner to verify availability.

This work is published by Samuel French, an imprint of Concord Theatricals Corp.

No one shall make any changes in this title(s) for the purpose of production. No part of this book may be reproduced, stored in a retrieval system, scanned, uploaded, or transmitted in any form, by any means, now known or yet to be invented, including mechanical, electronic, digital, photocopying, recording, videotaping, or otherwise, without the prior written permission of the publisher. No one shall share this title(s), or any part of this title(s), through any social media or file hosting websites.

For all inquiries regarding motion picture, television, online/digital and other media rights, please contact Concord Theatricals Corp.

THIRD-PARTY MATERIALS USE NOTE

Licensees are solely responsible for obtaining formal written permission from copyright owners to use copyrighted third-party materials (e.g., incidental music not provided in connection with a performance license, artworks, logos) in the performance of this play and are strongly cautioned to do so. If no such permission is obtained by the licensee, then the licensee must use only original materials and materials that the licensee owns and controls. Licensees are solely responsible and liable for clearances of all third-party copyrighted materials, and shall indemnify the copyright owners of the play(s) and their licensing agent, Concord Theatricals Corp., against any costs, expenses, losses and liabilities arising from the use of such copyrighted third-party materials by licensees. For music, please contact the appropriate music licensing authority in your territory for the rights to any incidental music not provided in connection with a performance license.

IMPORTANT BILLING AND CREDIT REQUIREMENTS

If you have obtained performance rights to this title, please refer to your licensing agreement for important billing and credit requirements.

TUCK EVERLASTING received its Broadway premiere on April 26, 2016 at the Broadhurst Theatre in New York. The performance was directed and choreographed by Casey Nicholaw, with scenic design by Walt Spangler, costume design by Gregg Barnes, lighting design by Kenneth Posner, sound design by Brian Ronan, hair design by Josh Marquette, and makeup design by Milagros Medina-Cerdeira. The production stage manager was Holly R. Coombs and the stage manager was McKenzie Murphy. The cast was as follows:

JESSE TUCK . . . . Andrew Keenan-Bolger

MAE TUCK . . . . Carolee Carmello

MILES TUCK . . . . Robert Lenzi

ANGUS TUCK . . . . Michael Park

WINNIE FOSTER . . . . Sarah Charles Lewis

MAN IN THE YELLOW SUIT . . . . Terrence Mann

MOTHER . . . . Valerie Wright

NANA . . . . Pippa Pearthree

HUGO . . . . Michael Wartella

CONSTABLE JOE . . . . Fred Applegate

ENSEMBLE . . . . Timothy J. Alex, Chloë Campbell, Ben Cook, Deanna Doyle, Brandon Espinoza, Lisa Gajda, Jessica Lee Goldyn, Neil Haskell, Justin Patterson, Marco Schittone, Jennifer Smith, Kathy Voytko, Sharrod Williams

CHARACTERS

JESSE TUCK

MAE TUCK

MILES TUCK

ANGUS TUCK

WINNIE FOSTER

MAN IN THE YELLOW SUIT

MOTHER

NANA

HUGO

CONSTABLE JOE

CARNY

ENSEMBLE – various memories, spirits, travelers, townsfolk, carnival workers, and patrons

SETTING

Treegap, New Hampshire and its surrounding wood

TIME

August 1893, with a few exceptions

AUTHOR'S NOTES

When incorporating an ensemble into your production, know that, as originally conceived, the chorus embodies much more than a band of "merry villagers." They will function as your audience's gateway into both Winnie Foster's and the Tuck family's past and futures, representing the passage of time, allowing us to fall into a character's memories as they come back to life around them, or present flashes of what the future may hold. The ensemble sings and dances as the physical expression of the joy and energy we all have when we are most alive and free.

"The Story of Winnie Foster," toward the end of the show, was originally conceived as a stylized ballet piece that expressed Winnie Foster's entire life, through fragments of her lifetime experiences; the stage directions set out the sequence, step-by-step. Although dance is our preferred way of telling Winnie's story, it is certainly not the only way; the important thing is that the characters of Winnie's life are brought back to life. Note that in the original production, there were six men, six women, and a small boy, cast in progressive ages to represent the different phases of Winnie's life: her children growing up, and herself growing old. You may make the ensemble bigger, of course, but it is most effective if you include a Winnie at age seventeen, a mature Winnie, and a Winnie in old age. Likewise, you'll want to cast different ensemble actors to embody her son's progression, from child to man, and her husband, Hugo, from boy to man to dearly departed spouse.

Whether you stage "The Story of Winnie Foster" as a ballet, a series of fixed tableaux, or a more ambitiously staged montage of wordless events, the crucial element is to illustrate the full (and finite) life that Winnie ultimately chooses to live, with weddings and births and deaths entwined in the community of people she loves, and who love her. That she "rode the wheel for all that it was worth."

ACT ONE

Scene One: The Spring

[MUSIC NO. 01 "OPENING"]

(A family of four crosses the stage to a bubbling spring at the base of a giant tree.)

JESSE. Come on, I think I see water up ahead!

MAE. Slow down, boys!

MILES. Are you kidding, Ma? We're dying of thirst!

> *(Each of the* **TUCKS** *–* **MAE** *[forties],* **ANGUS** *[forties],* **JESSE** *[seventeen], and* **MILES** *[twenty-one] – take a turn drinking.)*

ANGUS. This spring is a good omen. Where there's water, there's opportunity. And where there's opportunity, there's our new life. Let 1808 be our best year yet.

MAE. *(A toast.)* To the Tucks!

ALL THE TUCKS. To the Tucks!

> *(The lighting shifts.)*
>
> *(An ensemble of dancers swirls on stage.)*

ENSEMBLE MEN.
> DAY NA NA DAY NA NA DAY NA

ENSEMBLE.
> DAY NA NA DAY NA NA DAY NA
> AH AH AH AH

> *(The* **TUCKS** *exit.)*
>
> **(WINNIE FOSTER** *[eleven] enters; we are now in present day 1890s.)*

7

(She holds a green dress, but is wearing black mourning attire.)

[MUSIC NO. 02 "LIVE LIKE THIS"]

WINNIE.

TODAY IS THE DAY
I'VE BEEN WAITING FOREVER
IT'S THE FIRST DAY OF AUGUST 1893
TONIGHT THERE'S A FAIR
AND IF HANDLED JUST SO
I MIGHT GET MY MOTHER TO SAY I CAN GO

MOTHER. Winnie?

WINNIE. Coming, Mother!

GETTING OUT OF THE HOUSE
HAPPENS, WELL – *NEVER*
THERE'S A GATE AND A LOCK AND RULES TO ABIDE
I WISH I HAD WINGS
I'D LOOK GOOD WITH A PAIR
BUT IF WINGS ARE TOO MUCH, AT LEAST GIVE ME THE FAIR

LET THIS BE THE DAY
I STAY OUT ALL EVENING
AND FALL RIGHT INTO STEP
AS A BAND STARTS TO PLAY
NOT ANOTHER BORING DAY
IN TREEGAP NEW HAMPSHIRE
I CAN'T LIVE LIKE THIS
I CAN'T LIVE LIKE THIS FOREVER

ENSEMBLE.

DAY NA NA DAY NA NA DAY NA
DAY NA DAY NA NA

DAY NA NA DAY NA NA DAY NA
DAY NA DAY NA NA

(A chaise comes on piled with blankets. **MAE TUCK** *stands behind it.)*

MAE.

TODAY IS THE DAY

THE WAITING IS OVER
TONIGHT WE WILL ALL BE A FAMILY AGAIN
MY BOYS WILL BE HOME
BY THE END OF THE DAY
I CAN'T WAIT, I SHOULD WAIT, NO, I'LL MEET THEM
    HALFWAY

> (**MAE** *shakes the blankets. Her husband* **ANGUS** *is beneath.*)

Angus! Angus, wake up.

ANGUS. I'm up, I'm up. What's wrong?

MAE. Nothing's wrong! I just can't wait to see the boys!

ANGUS. So?

MAE. So, I'm going to meet them in Treegap Wood.

ANGUS. You sure that's a good idea, Mae?

MAE. Yes! Either I walk them home or they wring each other's necks.

ANGUS. Well, be careful.

MAE. I will! I love you, Angus.

> (**ANGUS** *begins to snore.*)

MAE.	ENSEMBLE.
LET THIS BE THE DAY	
I'M FREE OF THIS CABIN	I'M FREE
WHERE THE ONLY THING THAT MOVES	
IS THE CLOCK ON THE WALL	LET THIS BE THE DAY
BETTER OFF TO START THE HAUL	
TO TREEGAP NEW HAMPSHIRE	
I CAN'T LIVE LIKE THIS	LIVE LIKE THIS
I CAN'T LIVE LIKE THIS	LIVE LIKE THIS
FOREVER	

ENSEMBLE.

DAY NA NA DAY NA NA DAY NA
DAY NA DAY NA NA

(A train whistles. **MILES** *appears.)*

MILES.

OFF THE TRAIN IN NEW HAMPSHIRE
AND IT'S BACK IN AN INSTANT
THE FEELING THAT I'M SOMEWHERE I DON'T BELONG

(A silo rises from the floor. **JESSE** *is on top.)*

JESSE.

HELLO TREEGAP NEW HAMPSHIRE
CATCH ME UP ON WHAT'S NEW
YOUR SILO I SEE STILL HAS THE BEST VIEW

JESSE.	**MILES**.
I SWEAR	*(Echoing.)* I SWEAR

JESSE.

IS THERE ANYONE WHO STILL KNOWS ME?

MILES.	**JESSE**.
ALMOST THERE	*(Echoing.)* ALMOST THERE

MILES.

THIS TOWN NEVER OUTGROWS ME

JESSE.	**MILES**.
UNAWARE	*(Echoing.)* UNAWARE

MILES & JESSE.

I'LL NEVER KNOW WHY THIS WORLD CHOSE ME
TO LIVE LIKE THIS
LIVE LIKE THIS
LIVE LIKE THIS
FOREVER

(A **MAN IN YELLOW SUIT** *[sixties] enters.)*

MAN IN YELLOW SUIT.

TODAY A NEW TOWN
AND A NEW ONE TOMORROW
MY WHOLE LIFE EMPLOYED TO A TRAVELIN' FAIR
YOU MAY WONDER WHY
THIS OLD BARKER BARKS ON
IT'S THE TRAIL NO ONE KNOWS I HAVE STUMBLED UPON

MAN IN YELLOW SUIT.	ENSEMBLE.
LET THIS BE THE DAY	DAY NA NA DAY NA NA
THAT I LEARN THE SECRET	DAY NA NA DAY NA NA DAY
AND FIND WHO HOLDS THE KEY	DAY NA NA DAY NA NA
TO WHAT I'M LOOKING FOR	DAY NA NA DAY NA NA DAY NA

MAN IN YELLOW SUIT.

    I WILL KNOCK ON EVERY DOOR
    IN TREEGAP NEW HAMPSHIRE TO

MAN IN YELLOW SUIT.	MAE, JESSE & MILES.
	LIVE LIKE THIS
LIVE LIKE THIS	
	LIVE LIKE THIS
I COULD	
LIVE LIKE THIS	LIVE LIKE THIS

MAN IN YELLOW SUIT & MAE.

    FOREVER

        (WINNIE reappears – now wearing the green dress.)

WINNIE.	MAN IN YELLOW SUIT.
LET THIS BE THE DAY	
WHERE SOMETHING WILL HAPPEN	*(Echoing.)* SOMETHING WILL HAPPEN

WINNIE.	MAE.
LET ME SEE THE FAIR	*(Echoing.)* LET ME SEE MY BOYS

WINNIE.	MILES & JESSE.
LET MY MOTHER AGREE	*(Echoing.)* LET ME SEE

ALL.

    I FEEL IT COMING OVER ME
    IN TREEGAP NEW HAMPSHIRE
    I COULD LIVE LIKE THIS
    I COULD LIVE LIKE THIS
    LIVE LIKE THIS

W., MAE, J., MILES & YELLOW.	ENSEMBLE.
FOREVER	DAY NA NA DAY NA NA DAY NA
	DAY NA DAY NA NA
FOREVER	DAY NA NA DAY NA NA DAY NA
	DAY NA DAY NA NA

WINNIE & MAN IN YELLOW SUIT.
  I COULD

W., MAE, J., MILES & YELLOW.	ENSEMBLE.
LIVE LIKE THIS FOREVER	DAY NA NA DAY NA NA DAY NA

WINNIE & MAN IN YELLOW SUIT.
  I COULD

ALL.
  LIVE LIKE THIS

WINNIE, MAE, JESSE, MILES & YELLOW.
  FOREVER

ENSEMBLE.
  FOREVER

      (The song ends.)

      ***[MUSIC NO. 02A "LIVE LIKE THIS
      (PLAYOFF)"]***

WINNIE.	ENSEMBLE WOMEN.
LET THIS BE THE DAY	LET THIS BE THE DAY
WINNIE.	**ENSEMBLE MEN.**
LET THIS BE THE DAY	DAY NA NA DAY NA NA DAY NA
ENSEMBLE WOMEN.	
DAY NA NA DAY NA NA	
DAY NA	
LET THIS BE THE DAY	
	LET THIS BE THE DAY
	LET THIS BE THE
	LET THIS BE THE DAY

Scene Two: Foster Parlor

(WINNIE *steps into a sterile parlor.*)

(*Her* MOTHER, *Betsy Foster [late thirties], is in black mourning attire.*)

WINNIE. Okay, Mother. You can open your eyes...now!

(MOTHER *opens her eyes.*)

Surprise!

MOTHER. I don't understand.

WINNIE. I can't wear black to the Fair!

MOTHER. The Fair?

WINNIE. It's coming to town tonight. Can't we bend the rules? Just once?

(WINNIE*'s grandmother,* NANA *[seventies], awakens on a rocking chair.*)

NANA. *Surprise!*

WINNIE. You're late, Nana.

NANA. Oh. Did she say yes?

MOTHER. I'm sorry, you two, but no. It's not yet been a year since your father's funeral. And we can't be seen carrying on in public, as if nothing has happened.

WINNIE. But nothing does happen, not anymore.

MOTHER. Winnie, please march upstairs and put your proper attire back on.

NANA. Oh, Betsy –

WINNIE. I told you she would never let us have fun.

MOTHER. We have fun every day!

NANA. Keep your potato peeling, Betsy. We want cotton candy.

WINNIE. Father would have taken me to the Fair.

MOTHER. I know. But things are different now, and if you won't be a good girl for me, at least try to be a good girl for him.

[MUSIC NO. 03 "GOOD GIRL WINNIE FOSTER"]

WINNIE. Yes, Mother.

MOTHER. Good girl.

> (**MOTHER** *exits.*)

WINNIE.

> I'M TRAPPED IN A HOUSE OF SAD AND LONELY
> ON A STREET NAMED "MAIN" BUT YOU COULD CALL IT
>   "ONLY"
> IS IT RUDE TO SAY I'D VOLUNTEER
> FOR A DAY OF FUN JUST ONCE A YEAR?
> I'D FLY THE COOP IF ONLY I COULD
> BUT I'VE GOT A REALLY BAD CASE OF BEING GOOD
>
> I'D GO FIND TROUBLE IF THERE WAS SOME TO GET IN
> ASK A FRIEND TO PLAY, IF I HAD ONE TO LET IN
> NANA'S ROCKER SAWING THROUGH THE FLOOR
> EVERY DAY JUST LIKE THE ONE BEFORE
> WE LOCK OURSELVES BEHIND THAT DOOR
> IS IT WRONG TO WISH FOR SOMETHING MORE?

MOTHER. That's enough surprises for one morning.

> (*A croak fills the parlor.*)

Winnie, why did your dress just croak?

> (**WINNIE** *pulls a toad out of her pocket.*)

WINNIE. Meet my new friend, "Toad." I found him by the fence.

> (*Toad croaks in* **MOTHER***'s face.*)

MOTHER. Winnie, you know better than that! Take that filthy thing outside – where it belongs!

WINNIE. Yes, Mother.

NANA. Give him a kiss and see what happens!

> (*The house turns to take* **WINNIE** *outside.*)

Scene Three: Foster Garden

WINNIE.

GOOD GIRL WINNIE FOSTER
EVERY DAY
IS IN BED AT SEVEN
GOOD GIRL WINNIE FOSTER
EVERY DAY
IS A WELL BEHAVED ELEVEN
BUT SOME DAYS I WANT TO RAISE
A LITTLE SOMETHING MORE THAN HEAVEN

Well, Toad, we blew it.

(Toad croaks again.)

But at least it got us out of the house.

*(***WINNIE*** sets the toad down. It hops away.)*

ARE YOU FROM THE WOOD? I'M NOT ALLOWED THERE
BIG NEWS, I KNOW, I'M NOT ALLOWED ANYWHERE
WELL NOW'S YOUR CHANCE TO DISAPPEAR
GO HAVE FUN, I'LL BE RIGHT HERE
TIED TO A STRING LIKE A PRECIOUS PEARL
IT'S A PRETTY TIGHT LEASH FOR A REALLY GOOD GIRL

WINNIE.	**MOTHER/NANA/WOMEN.**
GOOD GIRL WINNIE FOSTER	WINNIE! WINNIE!
EVERY DAY	BE A GOOD GIRL WINNIE!
IS IN BED AT SEVEN	
	COME INSIDE!
GOOD GIRL WINNIE FOSTER	WINNIE! WINNIE!
EVERY DAY	BE A GOOD GIRL WINNIE!
IS A WELL-BEHAVED ELEVEN	
	COME INSIDE!
BUT SOME DAYS	WINNIE! WINNIE!
I WANNA RAISE	WINNIE! WINNIE!

WINNIE.

A LITTLE SOMETHING MORE THAN HEAVEN
SOME DAYS
I WANT TO RAISE
A LITTLE SOMETHING MORE THAN HEAVEN

(The song ends. **NANA** *appears at the front door.)*

NANA. Well, dear, I guess that's enough excitement for us today.

[MUSIC NO. 04 "JOIN THE PARADE"]

(Cymbals crash, trumpets blare. A rag-tag parade is led by the **MAN IN YELLOW SUIT**.*)*

MAN IN YELLOW SUIT & CARNIVAL BAND.

JOIN THE PARADE
FALL IN LINE FOR THE FAIR
BEFORE THE SUN SETS
BEFORE WE ROLL ON
LADIES AND GENTS
OUR MIDWAY PRESENTS
A TONIC FOR THE WOEBEGONE

MAN IN YELLOW SUIT.

COME TO THE FAIR
THE BEST DAY OF THE YEAR
THEY SAY IT WON'T LAST
YOUNG LADY THEY'RE RIGHT
A MERRIMENT MAKER
FILLING AN ACRE

MAN IN YELLOW SUIT & CARNIVAL BAND.

BUT THE TENT COMES DOWN TONIGHT

MAN IN YELLOW SUIT. Good morning!

WINNIE. It is now! The Fair is here!

MAN IN YELLOW SUIT. Well, now. Aren't you wise beyond your...

(He looks into her eyes.)

...eleven years, is it?

WINNIE. How did you guess?

MAN IN YELLOW SUIT. I'm a carnival man, young lady! (*Producing a coin from behind* **WINNIE**'s *ear.*) It's my business to know un-knowable things! Why, I can guess a girl's age just by looking into her eyes.

(*He moves on to* **NANA**.)

For instance, your sister here is probably eigh –

NANA. Ageless.

MAN IN YELLOW SUIT. Ageless, indeed. With the spunk of a schoolgirl.

NANA. I still feel like one! Why, I'd live forever, if I could.

MAN IN YELLOW SUIT. We have something in common. I'd do anything to live forever, and I do mean anything. Would you? Well, would you?

NANA. It was just an expression.

MAN IN YELLOW SUIT. To you, perhaps. Now, I don't suppose you've noticed anyone strange around here recently...

WINNIE. What do you mean, strange?

MAN IN YELLOW SUIT. Been up and down the state, looking for a highly unusual family. Used to live here in Treegap, some time ago.

NANA. I don't recall meeting anyone unusual. Until today.

(**MOTHER** *appears at the front door.*)

MOTHER. Pardon me, is there something I can help you with?

MAN IN YELLOW SUIT. No, pardon me. Just spreading the word about the Fair!

NANA. Is it as fun as it used to be?

MAN IN YELLOW SUIT. Madam, nothing's as fun as it used to be.

NANA. You can say that again.

MAN IN YELLOW SUIT. Nothing's as fun as it used to be.

(*Offstage, a music box is heard.*)

That tune! Do you hear it?

NANA. I've heard that very melody on and off my whole life. It's beautiful – and it always comes from our wood!

MAN IN YELLOW SUIT. Your wood, did you say?

MOTHER. Yes, she did.

MAN IN YELLOW SUIT. I'll keep that in mind. For now: much as I'd love to stay, ladies, a man only has so much time.

(He exits.)

NANA. Where do you find a suit that color – and why would you buy it?

WINNIE. Don't you see, Mother? It's a sign! We could go to the Fair, like we used to!

MOTHER. No – and that's the final word.

WINNIE. But Mother –

MOTHER. No more buts. The world can be a dangerous place, Winifred, and it is my job, alone, to protect you.

WINNIE. From what? Having fun?

MOTHER. That is enough. Now go inside and change your dress – and your attitude.

WINNIE. No! I hate you, and I hate your rules!

MOTHER. Winnie!

NANA. Betsy, let her be. She'll come in when she's ready to apologize.

[MUSIC NO. 05 "GOOD GIRL WINNIE FOSTER (TAG)"]

*(**MOTHER** and **NANA** go inside. Toad croaks at the fence.)*

WINNIE. Toad, you're back!

(Toad croaks.)

Why should I apologize? I don't want to just be "good." I want to be daring.

(Toad croaks again.)

I wish I could go with you.

WITH A CAGE FOR A YARD YOU CAN ONLY MOPE IN

WHEN A FRONT DOOR SHUTS, SHOULD A GATE OPEN?
IF I DON'T LEAVE NOW I'LL ONLY WISH I HAD
HOW CAN I KNOW GOOD WITHOUT TRYING BAD
TO THINK I'VE NEVER SEEN MY WOOD
I'VE GOT TO GET OUT
WHILE THE GETTING'S GOOD

> (**WINNIE** *runs from the yard as the scenery changes to reveal a mossy, mysterious wood.*)

ENSEMBLE.

DAY NA NA
DAY NA NA DAY NA

WINNIE. Toad, wait for me!

ENSEMBLE.

DAY NA NA
DAY NA NA DAY NA

Scene Four: The Spring

(In a clearing, at the same spring from the Prologue.)

ENSEMBLE.
  DAY NA
  DAY NA NA

WINNIE. *(Sing-song.)* Toad! Where are you?

> *(***JESSE*** *swings down from the tree and takes a drink of water.)*

> *(When he stands, he comes eye to eye with* **WINNIE.***)*

[MUSIC NO. 05A "JESSE AT THE SPRING"]

JESSE. Excuse me, are you lost?

WINNIE. That's exactly what I was going to ask.

JESSE. You shouldn't be here right now.

WINNIE. But these are my woods!

JESSE. I don't care whose woods these are, it's not safe for you to be here.

WINNIE. You're not old enough to boss me.

JESSE. Believe me. I am.

WINNIE. Oh, really. How old are you?

JESSE. Let's just say I'm…seventeen.

WINNIE. Oh. That is old.

JESSE. You have no idea.

> *(***WINNIE*** *brushes past* **JESSE.***)*

Uh, where do you think you're going?

WINNIE. I'm thirsty. I'm getting a drink from that spring, like you did.

JESSE. Oh no, you saw me drink? Look, you need to leave right now.

WINNIE. But it's just water!

JESSE. No, no, listen: When little girls drink from this spring, they turn into…

(The toad hops into view and croaks.)

Toads?

WINNIE. Nice try. I happen to know that toad. In fact, he's my toad.

JESSE. *Huh.* Well now that you say it, I do see the resemblance.

WINNIE. You're very odd.

(He puts out his hand.)

JESSE. I'm Jesse Tuck, how do.

WINNIE. Winnie Foster.

(They shake hands.)

I just ran away from home!

JESSE. And how's that going?

WINNIE. So far it's just a bunch of trees.

JESSE. Just a bunch of trees! You own these woods, Winnie Foster, and you don't even know what you've got! Come with me!

WINNIE. Where are we going?

JESSE. Up.

[MUSIC NO. 06 "TOP OF THE WORLD"]

WINNIE. Up, right now?

JESSE. There's no use running away if you don't make it an adventure!

WINNIE. Good point.

JESSE. I just hope you're not afraid of heights.

WINNIE. Only one way to find out!

(They begin climbing the tree.)

JESSE.
WATCH MY EVERY STEP
FIND A STURDY BRANCH
DON'T YOU DARE LOOK DOWN
PULL YOUR BODY UP
DIG IN YOUR HEELS

LET'S SEE
WHAT THIS TREE REVEALS

JUST A FEW MORE FEET
ALMOST AT THE TOP
WATCH THE ROBIN'S NEST
PULL YOUR BODY UP
'TIL YOU'VE BROKEN THROUGH
LET'S SEE
IF THIS TREE HAS A VIEW

AT THE TOP
AT THE TOP
AT THE TOP OF THE WORLD
YOU'RE DRAWING BACK A CURTAIN
AT THE TOP
AT THE TOP
AT THE TOP OF THE WORLD
THERE YOU KNOW FOR CERTAIN
YOU'RE ALIVE AND YOU ARE FREE
SO FOLLOW ME
TO THE TOP OF THE WORLD

WINNIE. Everything looks so different, up here!

JESSE. You ain't seen the half of it.

WINNIE. Don't you ever get afraid?

JESSE. If you aren't afraid, you aren't alive.

MOUNTAINS TO THE WEST
AN OCEAN TO THE EAST
A STORM CLOUD TO THE NORTH
READY TO POUR
EVERY SYCAMORE
LEAVES ME WANTING MORE AND MORE

AT THE TOP
AT THE TOP
AT THE TOP OF THE WORLD
MY HEAD AND HEART ARE POUNDING
AT THE TOP
AT THE TOP

AT THE TOP OF THE WORLD
I HEAR MY VOICE RESOUNDING
I'M ALIVE AND I AM FREE
SO LOOK AT ME

WINNIE.	ENSEMBLE.
YOU'VE GOTTA SEE IT TO BELIEVE IT	OOH

JESSE.

AND BELIEVE ME, I'VE SEEN IT	OOH
THE FRONTIER	OOH
OF THE UPPER ATMOSPHERE	

WINNIE.

A WONDER TO BEHOLD IT	OOH

JESSE.

A STORY YET UNTOLD,	OOH
IT'S UP HERE	AHH

WINNIE.

UP HERE

JESSE.

UP HERE	AHH

WINNIE.

UP HERE

WINNIE, JESSE & ENSEMBLE.

UP HERE!

JESSE.	ENSEMBLE.
I'LL GO OUT ON A LIMB	
WALK A TIGHTROPE WIRE	
FOR THE HIGHEST HEIGHT	
YES, I'LL RISK IT ALL	
GIVE ME A BARREL	
GUESS WHO'LL FIND A WATERFALL	AHH

ALL.

AT THE TOP
AT THE TOP

   AT THE TOP OF THE WORLD
WINNIE & JESSE.
   MY HEAD AND HEART ARE POUNDING
ALL.
   AT THE TOP
   AT THE TOP
   AT THE TOP OF THE WORLD
WINNIE & JESSE.   **ENSEMBLE.**
   I HEAR MY VOICE
      RESOUNDING
   I'M ALIVE AND I AM FREE
   SO LOOK AT ME...   AH AH AHH
   AT THE TOP   AH AH
   OF THE WORLD!

      (The song ends.)

      ***[MUSIC NO. 06A "MAE'S ENTRANCE
      TRANSITION"]***

Scene Five: The Spring

(MAE TUCK *paces, sits at the base of the tree, opens a music box.*)

(MILES *enters and shuts the music box.*)

MILES. Ma! Are you trying to get us caught out here?

MAE. You know me, Miles –

MILES. Nervous habit, I know.

MAE. Hey, can I have a proper hello, here?

(MAE *attempts a hug.*)

MILES. Great to see you, Ma. You're as pretty as ever.

MAE. And you don't look a day over 105.

MILES. Funny: sometimes I actually pray I'll wake up with gray hair and a pot belly.

MAE. Speaking of your father, he's back at the cabin, getting everything ready for your visit.

MILES. Come on, he always comes to meet us.

MAE. He isn't quite himself these days. But he'll snap back to life when he sees his boys.

MILES. And Jesse is running late, I assume?

MAE. It's been ten years since we've all been together, Miles. Another ten minutes won't kill us.

MILES. You got that right.

(JESSE *swings down from the tree.*)

JESSE. Ma!

MAE. Jesse! There's my sweet boy!
(They embrace.) The one who still hugs me.

JESSE. Listen! I have something I have to tell you.

MILES. Tell us at the cabin. You know this isn't a safe place to linger.

JESSE. Always great to be reunited, Miles!

MILES. I see you're still playing in trees.

JESSE. I see you still can't take a joke.

MAE. Boys. Jesse, you were telling me something?

JESSE. Right! So…hear me out. You know how you always say "good things come in small packages"?

(WINNIE jumps down from the tree.)

WINNIE. Hello!

JESSE. Not yet!

WINNIE. We climbed a tree! I saw the top of my house! It was great!

JESSE. She followed me here. Can we keep her?

MAE. A child? I always knew this day would come, that someone would discover us: but a child?

WINNIE. I thought you said they'd like me.

JESSE. She's not just a "child," she's also my friend.

MILES. Jesse, please tell me your friend doesn't know anything about the…you know.

WINNIE. Water?

JESSE. Oh, boy.

MILES. Jesse!

MAE. You told her about the water?

JESSE. This isn't my fault.

MILES. It never is. Ma, are you thinking what I'm thinking?

MAE. Unfortunately, yes.

(To **WINNIE.***)* Please know that, as a mother, I don't approve of what we're about to do.

(A beat. **MILES** *whips his coat off and over* **WINNIE***'s head, tossing her over his shoulder.)*

(She screams.)

Let's get her back to the cabin! Pa will know what to do.

JESSE. Winnie, are you okay?

(WINNIE screams again.)

*[MUSIC NO. 06B "KIDNAPPING
(TRANSITION)"]*

MAE. If she can scream, she can breathe!

JESSE. Don't worry, Winnie, we'll explain everything at home!

Scene Six: Foster Garden

(**HUGO** *[fifteen], shy and nervous, enters.*)

[MUSIC NO. 07 "HUGO'S FIRST CASE"]

HUGO.

BIG DAY
FIRST CASE
GIRL'S GONE
NO TRACE
SMALL TOWN
NO CRIME
NOW TREEGAP'S HIT THE BIG TIME

WHAT'S THIS
FRESH TRACKS
WHO'S THERE?
RELAX
FOOTPRINTS
SIZE NINE
A CLUE, YAHOO! NO, THOSE ARE MINE

NO DIRTY DEED GOES EXACTLY AS PLANNED LOOK
THAT'S WHAT IT SAYS IN MY DEPUTY HANDBOOK
EVEN THE BEST CROOK LEAVES YOU A CLUE
BIG DAY, FIRST CASE
GIRL'S GONE, NO TRACE
HUGO, YOU KNOW WHAT TO DO

> (*Trudging behind* **HUGO** *is* **CONSTABLE JOE**
> *[fifties].*)

CONSTABLE JOE. Hugo, there you are. I asked you not to get ahead of me. This being your first missing persons case, I recommend you keep your eyes open and your mouth closed. Shall we practice?

HUGO. No, I think I got it.

CONSTABLE JOE. See, that was a test. You just failed.

> (**MOTHER** *and* **NANA** *appear at their fence.*)

MOTHER. Joe!

CONSTABLE JOE. Betsy Foster! Got your message about Winnie and came as fast as we could.

NANA. Fast as molasses.

MOTHER. Mother, please. I'm so worried, Joe.

HUGO. We all are.

CONSTABLE JOE. Hugo! That annoying noise is Hugo trying to be my new deputy.

NANA. I feel safer already.

MOTHER. Hello, Hugo.

HUGO. Hello, Mrs. Foster. You look lovely, despite, well, everything.

CONSTABLE JOE. *(To* **MOTHER**, *re:* **HUGO**.*)* First day on the job.

MOTHER. Joe, Winnie's been gone since this morning. We found the gate wide open.

CONSTABLE JOE. *Huh.* Suspicious.

HUGO. Maybe she ran away.

CONSTABLE JOE. Hugo! When I want an opinion, I'll ask for one.

(Back to **MOTHER**.*)* Maybe she ran away.

MOTHER. Well, if she did, it's all my fault. I wouldn't even take her to the Fair.

CONSTABLE JOE. The Fair? Well, now, I don't mean to alarm you, but those people can be –

HUGO. Tricksy.

CONSTABLE JOE. Who?

HUGO. Tricksy. Meaning not to be trusted.

CONSTABLE JOE. Hugo!

(To **MOTHER**.*)* We'll have a good look around.

MOTHER. Find her, Joe. I can't bear the thought of losing anyone else.

CONSTABLE JOE. Don't worry, Betsy. I've got my best man on the case. Me!

(They begin to exit. **NANA** *has an epiphany.)*

NANA. If you hear a melody coming from our wood, follow
   that tune!

CONSTABLE JOE. Thanks for the tip, dear. Sounds like
   you've cracked the case.

>   (**MOTHER** *takes* **NANA** *inside as* **CONSTABLE JOE**
>   *exits.* **HUGO** *remains.*)

>   *[MUSIC NO. 07A "HUGO'S FIRST CASE
>   (REPRISE)"]*

HUGO.

>   HOUSE CALL
>   ADJOURNED
>   LEAVE NO STONE UNTURNED
>   FLIP HERE
>   FLIP THERE
>   THESE FLIPPING THINGS ARE EVERYWHERE
>
>   DON'T GIVE UP NOW, SEARCH CRANNY AND NOOK
>   THAT'S WHAT IT SAYS IN MY DEPUTY HANDBOOK
>   NO THAT'S NOT IT,
>   NO THAT'S MY LUNCH,
>   WHERE COULD IT BE?
>   BIG DAY
>   WHO TOOK
>   YOUNG GIRL
>   MY BOOK

>   (**CONSTABLE JOE** *re-enters and tosses the
>   "missing" handbook to* **HUGO**.)

CONSTABLE JOE. HUGO! Get a clue and let's get on with it.

>   (**CONSTABLE JOE** *exits again.*)

HUGO.

>   WILL YOU MAKE DEPUTY?

>   (**HUGO** *runs after* **CONSTABLE JOE**.)

Scene Seven: Tuck Cottage

[MUSIC NO. 07B "TUCK COTTAGE (TRANSITION)"]

(**MAE** *enters.*)

MAE. Angus, where are you? We're back! With a…surprise. Angus?

(**ANGUS** *snores from under the blankets.*)

Of course. Angus, wake up. Jesse met somebody at the spring.

(**ANGUS** *leaps up.*)

ANGUS. What? Do they know? Do they know the secret?

(**JESSE** *enters.*)

JESSE. Long time no see, Pa! Hope you're in a good mood!

ANGUS. Jesse! What have you gotten us into this time?

(**MILES** *enters, carrying* **WINNIE.**)

MILES. Here, Pa. It finally happened.

(**MILES** *spins* **WINNIE** *out of his jacket.*)

WINNIE. Please don't hurt me, please don't hurt me –

ANGUS. A child?

MAE. That's exactly what I said!

JESSE. Winnie, nobody's gonna hurt you.

WINNIE. I can't believe you tricked me. I trusted you.
    (As if they got engaged.) We climbed a tree!

ANGUS. Does she…does she…*you* know.

WINNIE. Know about the water?

MAE. Only that it's special! But she didn't drink any, so everything is fine!

JESSE. This is Winnie Foster. Winnie, this is my father, Angus. Usually, he's in clothes.

MAE. Not true.

ANGUS. A Foster! From Treegap? Your great-grandfather and I used to fish together! It's a pleasure to meet you! *(Puts out his hand.)* Don't you want to shake my hand?

WINNIE. No, I want to bite it. That's what my father told me to do if anybody ever tried to kidnap me.

ANGUS. Oh, no, Winnie. This isn't kidnapping.

MAE. Well, technically, honey.

JESSE. If you'd just let us explain –

MILES. That is a bad idea. As I've always said, if anybody finds out about us –

> *(***MILES*** *"slits his own throat" with his hand.)*

ANGUS. This is different, Miles. This is a child. A child changes everything.

> *(He puts his hand out – again.)*

Winnie Foster, I give you my word that we are not going to harm you.

(A beat.) Please don't bite me.

WINNIE. Fine. Can I please just go home?

MAE. Her mother must be worried sick.

MILES. This is ridiculous. So now what?

JESSE. Pa will know what to do! Right, Pa?

ANGUS. Of course I know what to do! Where are my boots?

> *(Finds them, looks down at his long johns.)*

Where are my pants?

MAE. Where are you going?

ANGUS. Fishing!

MAE. Fishing? Why!

ANGUS. We have a guest, we need a meal.

> *(Boots on, he runs upstairs.)*

MILES. So much for Pa knowing what to do.

JESSE. Miles, I am warning you…

MAE. Boys, let him go. I'm just happy to see him excited about something again. All that man's done for ten years is lie on the couch, waiting for you to come home.

(**ANGUS** *comes downstairs, grabs his fishing rod.*)

ANGUS. Welcome back boys. I've missed the sound of you fighting.

(*He exits.*)

WINNIE. You've been gone ten years? But you're only seventeen. I'm so confused.

JESSE. Oh, Ma, let's just tell her the truth about the water.

MILES. Oh, Ma, let's just not.

MAE. Miles, please.

JESSE. If Pa doesn't know what to do, that means it's up to us. Winnie, are you ready to hear the biggest secret ever?

MILES. The question is: is she ready to keep it? How do we know she won't run and tell everyone?

MAE. She knows too much now not to tell her everything. I guess we'll just have to trust her.

JESSE. Go ahead, Ma.

[MUSIC NO. 08 "THE STORY OF THE TUCKS"]

MAE.

ONCE UPON A TIME
ONCE UPON A TIME
CAN I START LIKE THAT?

MILES.

SHOULDN'T START LIKE THAT

MAE.

BE PATIENT WITH ME WINNIE
I'VE NEVER TOLD THIS BEFORE

ONCE THERE WAS A MAN
A MAN WITH A WIFE AND A FAMILY

JESSE.

    THAT'S MILES AND ME

MAE.

    JESSE LET ME TELL THE STORY
    I DON'T WANT TO START A WAR

    WE TORE FROM THE WEST
    TO SETTLE IN THE EAST
    LOOKING FOR A FARM OR SOME LAND AT LEAST

JESSE.

    GET TO THE PART WHERE I FALL FROM THE TREE

MILES.

    NO, YOU'VE GOT IT ALL WRONG

MAE.

    MILES! JESSE!
    THEN WE FOUND A WOOD

JESSE.

    YES WE FOUND A WOOD, CAN YOU GUESS WHICH WOOD?

WINNIE.

    MINE?

JESSE.

    YOU'RE GOOD.

MAE.

    WHERE WE FOUND OURSELVES A CLEARING
    AND CAMPED FOR THE NIGHT
    JUST THE FOUR OF US

MILES.

    PLUS THE CAT AND THE HORSE
    THEY PLAY A CRUCIAL PART

MAE.

    YES MILES, OF COURSE
    WE SLEPT BY A SPRING NEAR AN OLD ASH TREE

JESSE.

    AND THAT'S WHERE I CARVED A "T"

MAE.

    JESSE!

MILES.

> IN THE MORNING
> IN THE MORNING

MILES & JESSE.

> WE HAD NO WAY OF KNOWING
> WITHOUT EVEN THINKING

MILES, MAE & JESSE.

> WE DRANK FROM THE SPRING
> WHO KNEW THAT SPRING
> COULD CHANGE EVERYTHING

MAE.

> EXCEPT FOR THE HORSE
> EVERYBODY DRANK
> EVEN THE CAT

MILES.

> REMEMBER THAT

JESSE.

> YOU CAN LEAD A HORSE TO WATER –

MILES.

> I THINK SHE KNOWS THE PHRASE

MAE.

> SO DAYS WENT BY
> THEN MONTHS AND YEARS
> LIVED AN ORDINARY LIFE

MILES.

> SO IT APPEARS

MAE.

> THE OLD HORSE DIED AT TWENTY-FIVE

JESSE.

> BUT THE CAT WAS STILL ALIVE

MILES, MAE & JESSE.

> WE WEREN'T CHANGING
> WE WEREN'T GROWING
> WE HAD NO WAY OF KNOWING
> NOBODY WAS THINKING
> IT'S BECAUSE OF THE SPRING

WHO KNEW THAT SPRING
WOULD CHANGE EVERYTHING

MAE.	JESSE.	MILES.
THE TOWN BEGAN TO TALK	WINNIE, LOOK AT ME	
PEOPLE SHIED AWAY	WINNIE LISTEN HERE	
THEY WERE SO OUTRAGED		NO
WE HADN'T AGED		
OUR LIVES IMPIOUS	I SURVIVED A FREE FALL	LISTEN!
OUR LOOKS PERVERSE		
	HE SURVIVED MUCH WORSE	
		SHUT UP JESSE
STILL WE DIDN'T KNOW	YES OF COURSE WE KNEW	
DIDN'T KNOW THE SPRING	HOW COULD WE NOT KNOW	
WAS THE CAUSE OF IT		NO
OR WHERE WE'D SIT		
ON THE DELICATE BALANCE		
BETWEEN A BLESSING	THE GREATEST FAMILY	
AND A CURSE	IN THE UNIVERSE	DON'T CONFUSE THE GIRL

MILES, MAE & JESSE.

THE CAT AND THE HORSE
THE "T" ON THE TREE

THE DRINK THAT CHANGED US ETERNALLY
THAT'S OUR SECRET KEEP IT LOCKED UP TIGHT

WINNIE.

I STILL DON'T UNDERSTAND.

MILES.

ENOUGH! ALL RIGHT.
WE'RE NOT AGING
WE'RE NOT GROWING
AND NONE OF US KNOW WHY

ONCE UPON A TIME
WE DRANK FROM YOUR SPRING
AND NOW WE'LL NEVER DIE.

JESSE. And that's the story of the Tucks. The end.

MILES. The spring made us immortal.

WINNIE. Okay, I have a lot of questions, starting with: where is this cat?

MAE. He's the ultimate stray.

MILES. Every kitten for fifty miles has his little white paws.

WINNIE. How can I be sure you're not just telling me a story?

JESSE. Oh, that part's easy! Ma, where's my rifle? Winnie can shoot me!

(**JESSE** *runs off.*)

MAE. Nobody is shooting anybody, Jesse! I mean it, I just cleaned.

[MUSIC NO. 08A "MUSIC BOX"]

(*She sits and winds her music box.*)

WINNIE. It's true. That's the music box my Nana heard, back when she was my age…

(**MAE** *shuts it.*)

MAE. Oops.

(*The door swings open.* **ANGUS** *enters with an empty fishing rod.*)

ANGUS. Well, apparently I need Winnie's great-grandfather
   if I want to catch anyth –

JESSE. Found it!

> (JESSE *trips. His rifle goes off.* ANGUS, *shot, flips
> to the floor but then jumps up unharmed, rubbing
> his arm.*)

ANGUS. Dammit, Jesse!

MAE. Angus, please.

ANGUS. Aw, Mae, everyone swears when they get shot.

WINNIE. You shot your father.

MAE. Jesse, I told you. Not in the house.

> (WINNIE *is frozen in disbelief.*)

WINNIE. I don't understand! Didn't you get hurt?

ANGUS. Oh, honey, I'm fine.

JESSE. Nothing hurts us.

MILES. Not physically, anyway.

WINNIE. What else can you do? Can you fly?

JESSE. No.

MAE. But he certainly tried.

MILES. Headfirst.

WINNIE. It must be so fun to be you!

JESSE. It is!

MILES. Not exactly.

MAE. Not at all. It's not fun to be without your boys for ten
   years at a time.

WINNIE. Why do you spend so much time apart?

ANGUS. If we're seen together for too long, people start to
   realize we don't age.

MILES. It tends to scare the locals.

WINNIE. You could never scare me. But now I have about a
   million more questions.

MAE. I think that's enough for one night. Her mother must be frantic. I'd be willing to take her back home, right now.

ANGUS. At this hour? The poor girl must be exhausted. And she thinks we're fun!

WINNIE. Can I stay? Please?

MAE. I don't know. I don't think it's right to keep her overnight.

ANGUS. We'll take you back first thing in the morning, you have my word.

MILES. What we need, Pa, is her word. Winnie, do you swear you won't breathe a thing about us to anyone, ever?

MAE. She can sleep on it. Now let's get you out of that scratchy dress.

WINNIE. You could tell my dress was scratchy?

MAE. Mothers can always tell. Let's find you something in the attic.

(MAE and WINNIE exit.)

MILES. Look, I hate to be the voice of reason, but if the wrong person finds out about the water, they could play God with it. Or worse.

JESSE. Stop. She's just a kid. Don't make any good thing seem like it's the end of the world.

MILES. Easy to say when you've never looked out for anyone but yourself.

JESSE. That's what you think of me?

MILES. Who says I think of you?

(He goes to exit, but turns back.)

I shouldn't have implied that you're always selfish. You were an amazing uncle. Sometimes I think about that.

(MILES exits.)

ANGUS. Not natural, how much that boy has lost.

JESSE. He's not the only one. I used to have a brother.

ANGUS. You'll always have a brother. Now come on, while we got a minute, tell me everything, from the day you left.

JESSE. You sure, Pa? Gambling? Bar fights?

ANGUS. Jesse, I don't get out much. Don't skip a thing!

(*They exit.*)

[*MUSIC NO. 09 "INTO THE ATTIC"*]

Scene Eight: Tuck Attic

(A stairwell leads up to a cluttered crawl space.)

MAE. Oh, this attic is an embarrassment. I've had a hundred years to tidy it up, but when you never have guests, why clean?

WINNIE. We never have guests and we do nothing but clean. But Mother says "good girls" don't complain about chores.

MAE. I like your mother.

WINNIE. Don't tell anyone, but so do I.

MAE. Oh, it is so nice to talk to a girl, for once. What I'd give to have a daughter.

WINNIE. I'm not so sure you'd want me.

MAE. Why would you say that?

WINNIE. Before I ran away, I told my mother I hated her.

MAE. She didn't believe it for a second.

WINNIE. Are you sure?

MAE. Cross my heart. Now, rummage through that trunk, see what you find.

(WINNIE pulls out a pair of boy's trousers.)

WINNIE. How about…these!

MAE. Well, look at those.

WINNIE. I'll wear those if you wear…this!

(WINNIE pulls out a flowing silk dress.)

MAE. Oh, goodness.

WINNIE. It's beautiful! Was it yours?

MAE. Still is. And I bet it still fits. Between you and me, I think the water was good for my figure.

WINNIE. Was it a special dress?

MAE. I wore it the night Angus asked me to marry him. We went dancing, to our village hall, with musicians playing in the corner and wildflowers on the tables. We danced all night until the floors shook. That man used to love to dance. I miss him.

WINNIE. My father couldn't dance at all, but that didn't stop him from trying!

MAE. Isn't it nice when a memory makes you smile?

WINNIE. It is – but what if I start to forget it?

> *[MUSIC NO. 10 "MY MOST BEAUTIFUL DAY"]*

MAE. Impossible. Besides – your best memories haven't even happened yet.

WINNIE. You think?

MAE. I know.

> EVERY GROWN WOMAN
> WHO STANDS AT A MIRROR
> REMEMBERS ONE BEAUTIFUL DAY
> EVERY GIRL PAST HER PRIME
> KNOWS THE DATE AND THE TIME
> SHE LOOKED MOST EXQUISITE
> AND SHE WILL REVISIT
> REVISIT, REVISIT THAT DAY
> HER MOST BEAUTIFUL DAY
> FOR THE REST OF HER LIFE
>
> MY MOST BEAUTIFUL DAY
> PA TOOK ME DANCING
> AND EVERYTHING FELL INTO PLACE
> MY HAIR TIED LIKE SO
> WITH A BLACKBERRY BOW
> A NIGHT IN NOVEMBER
> THAT I WILL REMEMBER
> REMEMBER, REMEMBER THAT DAY
> MY MOST BEAUTIFUL DAY
> FOR THE REST OF MY LIFE

> (**MAE** *puts the dress on.*)

> EACH MEMORY
> A SWEET MELODY
> YOUR HEART CLINGS TO

WITH EACH PASSING DAY
WHAT TIME TAKES AWAY
THE HEART MAKES NEW
LOOKING BACK, LOOKING BACK
IS SOMETHING TO LOOK FORWARD TO
YOUR MOST BEAUTIFUL DAY
FOR THE REST OF YOUR LIFE

(**ENSEMBLE** *enters, swirling* **MAE** *back in time.* **ANGUS** *appears and gives* **MAE** *the music box.*)

[MUSIC NO. 10A "BEAUTIFUL DAY (PART 2)"]

(*He gets down on one knee.*)

ANGUS.

APRIL MAY JUNE JULY
A SUNDAY WHEN THE CHAPEL'S FREE
TRUE LOVE IS IN SHORT SUPPLY
DARLING MAE, MARRY ME?

(**MAE** *nods "yes" and* **ANGUS** *takes her into his arms. Everyone dances in celebration.*)

MAE.

EACH MEMORY
A SWEET MELODY
YOUR HEART CLINGS TO
WITH EACH PASSING DAY
WHAT TIME TAKES AWAY
THE HEART MAKES NEW
LOOKING BACK, LOOKING BACK
IS SOMETHING TO LOOK FORWARD TO
YOUR MOST BEAUTIFUL DAY
FOR THE REST OF YOUR LIFE

(**ENSEMBLE** *exits. We segue back to Tuck cottage.*)

YOUR MOST BEAUTIFUL DAY
FOR THE REST OF YOUR LIFE

(**WINNIE** *is now dressed in the boy's clothes. She hugs* **MAE**.)

WINNIE. What happens now?

MAE. Bed happens now. For all of us.

(**MAE** *sets up a makeshift bed.*)

WINNIE. You expect me to fall asleep, after everything that happened today?

MAE. I know how you feel. We haven't had this much excitement for as far back as I can remember. But try to get some rest.

WINNIE. I will.

MAE. I'll see you first thing tomorrow morning.

(**MAE** *starts to exit.*)

WINNIE. Mae?

MAE. Yes?

WINNIE. Am I safe up here?

MAE. The safest. I promise. Good night, Winnie.

WINNIE. Good night.

[MUSIC NO. 10B "FROM ATTIC TO PORCH"]

(**MAE** *exits.*)

A NIGHT IN A HOUSE THAT'S CLEARLY HAUNTED
THAT'S THE PRICE YOU PAY, GETTING WHAT YOU WANTED
ONE SMALL STEP OUTSIDE YOUR DOOR
LANDS YOU WIDE AWAKE ON AN ATTIC FLOOR
NOT QUITE WHAT I HAD BARGAINED FOR
AND YET I'D TAKE A LITTLE MORE

(**JESSE** *pops up at the window.*)

(*Music stops.*)

JESSE. Boo!

WINNIE. Ahh, Jesse! Unlike you, some of us can actually be scared to death.

JESSE. Sorry! It's just: I couldn't sleep, so I was thinking of going on a secret adventure.
(*A beat.*) Anyway, sleep tight!

(*He starts to go.*)

WINNIE. Wait, wait! What kind of adventure?

JESSE. Any kind you want. The first rule of sneaking out is: do whatever your parents would say no to.

WINNIE. That would be the Fair. Jesse! Can we go to the Fair?

JESSE. Excellent choice!

WINNIE. So what's the plan?

JESSE. You climb out the window.

(Music resumes.)

I'll meet you downstairs.

WINNIE. Why aren't you coming with me?

JESSE. Because the second rule of sneaking out is: we need to wear disguises.

WINNIE. Sounds good!

JESSE. Wait, Winnie!

(She's already gone out the window.)

The third rule is don't get caught!

(JESSE *exits downstairs as the stage revolves to reveal the front porch.)*

Scene Nine: Tuck Porch

(**ANGUS** *sits on the porch holding a fishing rod.*)

(**WINNIE** *bounds past him.*)

ANGUS. Going somewhere?

(*She freezes.*)

WINNIE. Nowhere special.

ANGUS. Mm-hmm.

(**WINNIE** *notices* **ANGUS***'s fishing pole.*)

WINNIE. Um…Mr. Tuck?

ANGUS. Call me Angus.

WINNIE. Okay. Mr. Angus, you do know that in order to actually catch a fish, you need water, right?

ANGUS. Good tip. Now, I'm out here working on my technique. What's your alibi?

WINNIE. My alibi?

ANGUS. That's Latin for: why are you sneaking out of my house?

WINNIE. Oh! I was just getting some fresh air!

ANGUS. I bet you are. One, two –

(*On "three,"* **JESSE** *barrels out, wearing a cap.*)

JESSE. Come on, let's go before we're –

ANGUS. (*To* **WINNIE.**) This must be your fresh air.

JESSE. Oh, Pa. I know what this looks like, but-but-but –

ANGUS. This oughta be good.

WINNIE. He's taking me to the Fair!

ANGUS. Oh, he is, is he?

JESSE. Please, Pa. She's our guest, the least I can do is show her a good time.

ANGUS. Your mother wouldn't like this.

JESSE. Don't think about that right now. Think about… funnel cakes! And carnival games!

(*A beat.*)

ANGUS. Well, now I want to go.

WINNIE. My father used to love the Fair, too.

ANGUS. What do you mean, he "used to" – *(Realizing.)* Oh.

JESSE. *(Taking off his cap.)* Winnie.

ANGUS. Go. Both of you.

WINNIE. You mean it?

ANGUS. I mean it. Have some fun, for old times' sake.

(To **JESSE.***)* As long as you keep an extra low profile.

JESSE. Yesss!

*(***JESSE** *goes to hug him.* **ANGUS** *backs away.)*

ANGUS. Get outta here! Before you-know-who catches me catching you. And I get in trouble.

*(***JESSE** *grabs* **WINNIE***'s hand to exit, but she turns back around.)*

WINNIE. Thank you, Mr. Angus!

(They exit.)

ANGUS. Bring me back a funnel cake!

Scene Ten: The Fair

(*The* **MAN IN YELLOW SUIT** *enters the fairground.*
The Fair comes to life.)

[MUSIC NO. 11 "JOIN THE PARADE"]

MAN IN YELLOW SUIT & ENSEMBLE.

JOIN THE PARADE
FALL IN LINE FOR THE FAIR
BEFORE THE SUN SETS
BEFORE WE ROLL ON
LADIES AND GENTS
OUR MIDWAY PRESENTS
A TONIC FOR THE WOEBEGONE

MAN IN YELLOW SUIT.

COME TO THE FAIR
THE BEST DAY OF THE YEAR
THEY SAY IT WON'T LAST
AND SONNY THEY'RE RIGHT
A MERRIMENT MAKER FILLING AN ACRE

MAN IN YELLOW SUIT & ENSEMBLE.

BUT THE TENT COMES DOWN TONIGHT

(**WINNIE** *and* **JESSE** *enter, holding cotton candy.*)

WINNIE. Wow, it's even better than I remembered! Jesse, I am so glad we snuck out!

JESSE. Am I good, or am I good?

WINNIE. You're the best! What do you think we should try next?

JESSE. You lead the way this time, kid. I think I've been everywhere in the world except the Fair.

WINNIE. Everywhere?

[MUSIC NO. 12 "PARTNER IN CRIME"]

JESSE. Well, almost everywhere.

THE PYRAMIDS, THE BROOKLYN BRIDGE
THE RIO GRANDE, THE RHINE
I'VE SEEN THE SEVEN WONDERS OF THE WORLD

CAN'T WAIT FOR EIGHT AND NINE
BUT BECAUSE OF MY PREDICAMENT
MY PECULIAR SITUATION
TO KEEP MY PROFILE LOW, LOW, LOW
I'M A ONE-MAN OPERATION

WINNIE. Jesse, I've got it!

YOU NEED A PARTNER IN CRIME
SOMEONE TO SHARE IN THE VIEW
WHY SEE THE WORLD AND ALL OF ITS GLORIES
WITHOUT A FRIEND TO TELL YOUR STORIES TO?

JESSE.

SOMEONE TO STAND AT MY SIDE
TWO EXTRA FISTS IN A FIGHT
WHY SHOULD THE ROAD BE LONG AND LONELY?

WINNIE.

WHY NOT TEAM UP?

JESSE & WINNIE.

WE'VE ONLY GOT TONIGHT

JESSE.

IF NO ONE'S THERE TO HEAR IT
DOES A FALLING TREE MAKE SOUND?

WINNIE.

ARE WE HEARD, OR SEEN, OR ANYTHING
WITHOUT A FRIEND AROUND?

JESSE.

THE OLD GREAT WALL, THE TAJ MAHAL
YES, THEY ALL HAVE MERIT

WINNIE.

BUT THIS TRAVELIN' FAIR COULD TAKE THE CAKE
BECAUSE YOU GET TO SHARE IT

JESSE. *(Offering* **WINNIE** *a sample of the cake he just pilfered.)*
Carrot?

WINNIE.	**JESSE.**
YOU NEED A PARTNER IN CRIME	*(Echoing.)* I NEED A PARTNER IN CRIME
SOMEONE TO SHARE IN A LAUGH	*(Echoing.)* SOMEONE TO SHARE IN A LAUGH

WINNIE.

RUNNING A RACE WITHOUT A PACE SETTER

JESSE.

I'M OUT OF PLACE

JESSE & WINNIE.

WITHOUT MY BETTER HALF

*(**WINNIE** and **JESSE** disappear into the stalls.)*

CARNY. Feed the hungry clown, feed the hungry clown! Three out of five wins a prize.

*(**CONSTABLE JOE** and **HUGO** appear and approach the carny.)*

CONSTABLE JOE. Say, you see a little girl?

CARNY. What do you think? It's a Fair.

CONSTABLE JOE. Smart aleck. C'mon, Hugo, let's look over there.

JESSE & WINNIE.

WITH YOU

JESSE.

THE FUN IS TWO FOR ONE

WINNIE.

AND CHOCK FULL OF SURPRISES

JESSE & WINNIE.

WITH YOU

WINNIE.

THE LINE MOVES TWICE AS FAST

JESSE & WINNIE.

AND NO ONE REALIZES

JESSE.

WITH TWO WHATEVER WE DO NOW
WILL MERIT REMINISCING

JESSE & WINNIE.

WITH TWO I FINALLY FEEL SOMEHOW
THAT SOMETHING ISN'T MISSING

JESSE & WINNIE.	**ENSEMBLE.**
I HAVE A PARTNER IN CRIME	*(Echoing.)* A PARTNER IN CRIME

JESSE & WINNIE.
> SOMEONE TO SHARE IN THE VIEW

JESSE, WINNIE & ENSEMBLE.
> WHY SEE THE WORLD AND ALL OF ITS GLORIES
> WITHOUT A FRIEND TO TELL YOUR STORIES TO?

ENSEMBLE.
> LAST CHANCE FOR FUN AT THE FAIR
> SUN'S SETTING TOMORROW WE'RE GONE

> ### [MUSIC NO. 12A "PARTNER IN CRIME (PART 2)"]

> *(Dance break.)*

JESSE, WINNIE & ENSEMBLE.
> YOU NEED A PARTNER
> A PARTNER IN CRIME
> TWO EXTRA FISTS IN A FIGHT
> STUCK IN A STICKY SITUATION
> LUCKY THE TRICK'S COLLABORATION
> WHY SHOULD THE ROAD BE LONG AND LONELY?

JESSE & WINNIE.
> WE'VE ONLY GOT TONIGHT

ENSEMBLE.
> LAST CHANCE FOR FUN AT THE FAIR

JESSE & WINNIE.
> A PARTNER IN CRIME

ENSEMBLE.
> SUN'S SETTING TOMORROW WE'RE GONE

JESSE, WINNIE & ENSEMBLE.
> MY PARTNER IN CRIME!

> *(At song's end, the crowd disperses.)*

> ### [MUSIC NO. 12B "PARTNER IN CRIME (PLAYOFF)"]

JESSE. Okay, "partner," what's next on the list?

WINNIE. Well, I wasn't gonna say anything, but you haven't won me anything yet!

JESSE. Hey, now! Them's fightin' words!

(The **MAN IN YELLOW SUIT** *bursts forth.)*

MAN IN YELLOW SUIT. Step right up, step right up! Last game of the night! Last chance to play Fool the Guesser! I guess your age wrong, you win a prize!

WINNIE. Oh, my gosh. It's that man. Jesse, you don't want to play this game, believe me.

JESSE. You're not leaving here without a prize. Watch this.

*(***JESSE** *breaks away, but* **WINNIE** *stays back.)*

MAN IN YELLOW SUIT. Come, now! Well, if no one's brave enough…

JESSE. Bet you can't guess my age, sir!

WINNIE. Jesse, wait –

JESSE. Relax, Winnie. Joke's on him.

WINNIE. Jesse, no!

(The **MAN IN YELLOW SUIT** *notices* **WINNIE.***)*

MAN IN YELLOW SUIT. Well, whaddya know. It's that eleven-year-old spitfire from this morning. Let's see if your friend's age is as easy to guess as yours was!

(He sizes **JESSE** *up.)*

Examine the height, consider the shoe size – but the answer is always in the eyes. Yessiree, the age is always in the –

(The **MAN IN YELLOW SUIT** *backs up, startled.)*

JESSE. Well?

MAN IN YELLOW SUIT. *(Recovering.)* Seventeen! Am I right?

*(***WINNIE** *crosses to pull* **JESSE** *away.)*

WINNIE. That's it! You got it on the first try.

MAN IN YELLOW SUIT. Wait, wait a minute. How old are you really?

*(***JESSE** *squirms away, but the* **MAN IN YELLOW SUIT** *looks deeper into his eyes.)*

JESSE. Seventeen, just like you guessed.

MAN IN YELLOW SUIT. Of course, I'm never wrong! And I always quit when I'm on top! That's all, folks! Thanks for coming. Good night!

JESSE. Yes, good night.

MAN IN YELLOW SUIT. Hey, seventeen, you're not going to let your little friend go home without a prize, now, are you?

> (*The* **MAN IN YELLOW SUIT** *pulls* **WINNIE** *across the stage.* **JESSE** *follows. The* **MAN IN YELLOW SUIT** *hands a doll to* **WINNIE**.)

How about this prize, girly? You like it?

WINNIE. Yes, thank you.

> (*The* **MAN IN YELLOW SUIT** *pulls a knife on* **JESSE**.)

MAN IN YELLOW SUIT. And how about this prize, old man. You like it?

JESSE. Run, Winnie! Go!

> (**WINNIE** *dashes through the crowd.*)

MAN IN YELLOW SUIT. Just want to ask you a few questions, is all.

> (*The* **MAN IN YELLOW SUIT** *leans in closer with the knife.*)

JESSE. You don't scare me.

MAN IN YELLOW SUIT. Oh, really? 'Cause you sure look scared.

[MUSIC NO. 12C "RUN TO THE SILO"]

> (*Defiant,* **JESSE** *grabs the knife and pulls it into his gut.*)

JESSE. Ha!

> (*The* **MAN IN YELLOW SUIT** *is dazzled.*)

MAN IN YELLOW SUIT. It's you! It's actually you!

> (**JESSE** *pulls the knife out and runs through the crowd, causing a stir.*)

(The CONSTABLE *and* HUGO *reappear.)*

CONSTABLE JOE. What's going on here?

MAN IN YELLOW SUIT. It's – it's nothing! Just a little misunderstanding!

> *(The* MAN IN YELLOW SUIT *runs off.* HUGO *starts off in the other direction.)*

CONSTABLE JOE. Hugo, where are you going? I smell a rat.

HUGO. Forget the rat, we have to find Winnie. Come on!

> *(*HUGO *exits, leaving* CONSTABLE JOE *behind.)*

CONSTABLE JOE. I'm already ahead of you, Hugo. Wait up!

Scene Eleven: The Silo

(JESSE *and* WINNIE *are revealed on the silo.*)

WINNIE. I was so afraid you wouldn't get away.

JESSE. I may be 102 but I can still outrun anyone.

WINNIE. I'm so sorry. I tried to warn you.

JESSE. No, no. It's okay. It's refreshing to have somebody looking out for me who isn't Ma.

WINNIE. But Jesse, that man came by my house this morning. He heard the music box. He…knows about you.

JESSE. I know he knows. Guess the family reunion's over early. It won't be the first time.

WINNIE. But you just got here. And you're the first real friend I've made in –

JESSE. Forever?

WINNIE. Yes.

JESSE. Believe me, I know.

WINNIE. So, is this goodbye, then?

JESSE. Maybe not. Listen: Ma and Pa and Miles? They don't know how to enjoy anything anymore. They're stuck in the past. But you?

[MUSIC NO. 13 "SEVENTEEN"]

You thought it was amazing to climb a tree. Imagine seeing the Eiffel Tower! The Egyptian pyramids!

WINNIE. *The world.*

JESSE. Exactly.

WINNIE. But Jesse, I'm not even allowed to play in the woods. I could never go on those kinds of adventures.

JESSE. Don't worry. I've got that figured out.

SIX YEARS FROM NOW
YOU WILL TURN SEVENTEEN
TURN SEVENTEEN
THE SAME AGE AS ME
SIX YEARS FROM NOW

    GO TO THE SPRING
    GO TO THE SPRING
    AND DRINK

    I'LL WAIT FOR YOU
    'TIL YOU TURN SEVENTEEN
    TURN SEVENTEEN
    THE SAME AGE AS ME
    SIX YEARS FROM NOW
    GO TO THE SPRING
    GO TO THE SPRING
    AND DRINK

WINNIE. What if I forget where the spring is?

JESSE. I'll go get some of the water, and you can take it back and keep it – safe.

WINNIE. You make the world sound so exciting, I want to just drink the water right now.

JESSE. No! You have to wait.

WINNIE. Why? What's the difference?

JESSE. You'll see. There's a difference.
    WINNIE WAIT WITH ME
    AND WE COULD BE MARRIED
    WINNIE WAIT WITH ME
    AND WE'LL SHARE THE WORLD
    WINNIE YOU CAN STOP TIME
    AND LIVE LIKE THIS FOREVER

      (*The* **MAN IN YELLOW SUIT** *enters, spots* **JESSE** *and* **WINNIE.**)

      [MUSIC NO. 14 "END OF ACT I"]

ENSEMBLE.	**MAN IN YELLOW SUIT.**
DAY NA NA	Finally!
DAY NA NA	
DAY NA	
DAY NA	
DAY NA NA	
	I COULD

DAY NA NA	LIVE LIKE THIS
DAY NA NA	FOREVER
DAY NA	

JESSE.

DAY NA	LIVE LIKE THIS
DAY NA NA	FOREVER

JESSE, WINNIE, MAN IN YELLOW SUIT & ENSEMBLE.

LIVE LIKE THIS

JESSE. So what do you say, Winnie? Do you want to live forever?

JESSE, WINNIE, MAN IN YELLOW SUIT & ENSEMBLE.

FOREVER!

(Blackout.)

ACT TWO

Scene One: Backstage At The Fair

[MUSIC NO. 15 "ENTR'ACTE"]

(The next day.)

MAN IN YELLOW SUIT. It's water! And it's in the wood!

[MUSIC NO. 16 "EVERYTHING'S GOLDEN]

Now this is what I call a good morning! I can leave the Fair now that I found the real freaks!

LOOK WHO HAS A SPRING IN HIS STEP
IT'S TRUE THERE'S A BOUNCE IN EACH TOE
THIS HAS-BEEN FEELS YOUNG AGAIN
JUST WHEN HE WAS USED TO FEELIN' OLD

(The **ENSEMBLE** *appears.)*

FELLOW TAKE A LOOK AT MY SUIT
YELLOW HAS ACQUIRED A GLOW
FLEA BAGS CAN LAUGH AND JOKE
THESE RAGS WILL BE SPINNIN' INTO GOLD

GOLDEN LIKE THE SUN
RISING IN THE EAST
GOLDEN WITH THAT BRAND NEW DAY SHINE
GOLDEN LIKE THE YEARS
IT TOOK TO GET ME HERE
SOON EVERYTHING'S GOLDEN
AND EVERYTHING'S MINE

I'm gonna be the richest son of a gun of all time. Who wouldn't pay a fortune for a sip of forever?

NUTSHELL: WHEN THE WATER IS MINE
DON'T TELL ME YOU WOULDN'T BUY
MY MERCHANDISE, I'LL NAME THE PRICE
AND MAKE A KILLING MAKING SURE YOU NEVER DIE

MY PURPOSE, MY PLAN, MY WHOLE RAISON D'ETRE
STRIKE IT RICH AND RULE THE WORLD, ET CETERA ET
    CET'RA
AND OF COURSE BECOME IMMORTAL SOMEWHERE 'LONG
    THE WAY
I'LL BE

ENSEMBLE.

GOLDEN LIKE THE SUN

MAN IN YELLOW SUIT.

GOLDEN LIKE MY SUIT	**ENSEMBLE.**
GOLDEN WITH THAT	
BRAND NEW DAY SHINE	BRAND NEW DAY SHINE
GOLDEN LIKE THE YEARS	
IT TOOK TO GET ME HERE	
SOON	

ALL.

EVERYTHING'S GOLDEN

MAN IN YELLOW SUIT.

AND EVERYTHING'S MINE

*[MUSIC NO. 16A "EVERYTHING'S GOLDEN
(PART 2)"]*

Come on, girls. One last dance, and then I'm off to
make my millions.

(Dance break.)

MAN IN YELLOW SUIT.	**ENSEMBLE.**
GOLDEN LIKE THE SUN	EVERYTHING'S GOLDEN
	EVERYTHING'S GOLDEN
GOLDEN LIKE MY SUIT	
	EVERYTHING'S GOLDEN
GOLDEN WITH THAT	
BRAND NEW DAY SHINE	

GOLDEN LIKE THE YEARS
IT TOOK TO GET ME HERE
SOON EVERYTHING'S
    GOLDEN

EVERYTHING'S
GOLDEN
EVERYTHING'S GOLDEN

EVERYTHING'S GOLDEN

EVERYTHING'S GOLDEN
    AND EVERYTHING'S

ENSEMBLE.
    MINE

MAN IN YELLOW SUIT.
    AND EVERYTHING'S

ENSEMBLE.
    MINE

MAN IN YELLOW SUIT.
    AND EVERYTHING'S MINE!

    (The number ends.)

Goodbye now!

    [MUSIC NO. 16B "EVERYTHING'S GOLDEN (PLAYOFF)"]

See you in the next life – or maybe I won't!

    (He travels to the Foster house.)

EVERYTHING'S MINE
EVERYTHING'S MINE
EVERYTHING'S MINE
EVERYTHING'S

Hellloooo. Knock knock!

Scene Two: Foster Fence

(**MOTHER** *and* NANA *come to their fence.*)

MAN IN YELLOW SUIT. I know where your daughter is.

(*All three exit into the Foster house.*)

Scene Three: Tuck Cottage

(**WINNIE** *wakes on* **ANGUS**'s *chaise in the living room.*)

[MUSIC NO. 17 "SEVENTEEN (REPRISE)"]

WINNIE.
SIX YEARS FROM NOW
I WILL TURN SEVENTEEN
TURN SEVENTEEN
AND DRINK FROM THE SPRING
SIX YEARS FROM NOW
I WILL GO TO THE SPRING
GO TO THE SPRING
AND DRINK

Oh, I can't wait 'til I'm seventeen.

(**ANGUS** *enters.*)

ANGUS. Look who found the comfiest bed in the house!

WINNIE. Morning, Mr. Angus.

ANGUS. Mornin'. Did you get any sleep?

WINNIE. Not exactly.

(**JESSE** *enters.*)

ANGUS. Morning, Jesse. Can I make you kids some breakfast?

JESSE. I'll pass, thanks.

ANGUS. So? How was your big late night adventure?

JESSE. It was fine.

WINNIE. Jesse's being modest. It was the most fun I've had in at least a year, and –

JESSE. Winnie, cut it out.

WINNIE. What?

JESSE. You don't have to cover for me. Pa, I did something really stupid last night.

ANGUS. Give yourself some credit, son. You do something really stupid every day.

JESSE. No, Pa, take me seriously. Please. We met this…crazy carny at the Fair. Except he wasn't crazy.

ANGUS. Well, what was he?

JESSE. Dangerous. Scary. Pa, he knows about us.

ANGUS. Where is he now?

WINNIE. We lost him, I'm sure we did.

ANGUS. These woods are getting thinner every year. If he wanted to, he could track us down within a couple of days.

JESSE. So, what do we do?

ANGUS. First, we figure out how to break it to you-know-who.

(MAE *enters, holding* WINNIE*'s dress.*)

MAE. Here's your dress, sweetie. Let's get you changed, before Miles sees you in those clothes.

JESSE. Ma, I did something really stupid.

MAE. Well, that's a new record. I haven't even had breakfast.

ANGUS. We've got to pull up stakes, Mae.

MAE. What? What happened?

ANGUS. I just… I got a funny feeling, is all.

JESSE. Pa, stop. At least let me try to be a man and admit what I did.

MAE. Okay, now you're scaring me.

JESSE. I snuck out last night. There's a creepy man who saw my face. He knows the secret.

ANGUS. We've gotta split up. It's not safe, otherwise.

MAE. I can't believe this is happening. I've waited ten years for this visit.

ANGUS. We'll have to leave our cottage – maybe for good this time.

WINNIE. I could come with you!

MAE. No. Absolutely not. I knew I should have taken her back last night.

ANGUS. This is my fault. I never should have taken us to Treegap Wood in the first place.

WINNIE. But then you wouldn't have found the spring!

MAE. Honey, that's entirely his point.

WINNIE. But the spring is a miracle!

(WINNIE *keeps explaining, oblivious.*)

I'd drink from it right now – but Jesse wants me to wait.

(*Silence.* JESSE *sinks to the kitchen table.*)

MAE. Jesse Tuck, for the first time in 102 years, I am truly disappointed in you.

JESSE. But Ma –

MAE. No. Not this time. There are some things that even you can't sweet-talk your way out of.

(*She storms out to the porch.*)

ANGUS. Well, now you've upset your mother. Say your goodbyes.

(ANGUS *exits to* MAE.)

WINNIE. Did I do something wrong?

JESSE. Never.

WINNIE. Do you still mean what you said, at the silo? About the water I can keep 'til I'm seventeen?

(JESSE *looks up.*)

JESSE. I'll go get you some. But you have to put it somewhere safe, where no one will find it.

(MILES *enters.*)

MILES. Why don't I smell pancakes? The kid must be starving!

(MILES *sees* JESSE *before he sees* WINNIE.)

Where's Ma and Pa?

WINNIE. They're outside. I think I made them mad.

(*Now* MILES *spots* WINNIE.)

MILES. Why are you wearing those clothes?

(To JESSE.*)* Where did she get Thomas's clothes?

WINNIE. Who's Thomas?

(JESSE *stands.*)

JESSE. Don't let him bully you, Winnie – and you didn't make anyone mad. I did. Like always.

MILES. What did you do now, Jesse?

JESSE. I don't care who's disappointed in me, anymore. Someday, I want Winnie to drink the water.
(A beat.) Go ahead. Say it.

MILES. Jesse, even for you, this is a new level of selfish.

WINNIE. No, it's not! I want to see the Eiffel Tower! I want to see the Egyptian pyramids!

MILES. No, you want to see old age. You want to see your children grow up.

JESSE. I refuse to keep living alone in the shadows.

MILES. Jesse, if you won't listen to your big brother, then listen to some common sense. So, okay: your plan works for three years, maybe four if you're lucky – then what? Do you someday start a family, and make your children drink the water? And what about when the neighbors catch on to your secret? Then what? You wanna go to jail – forever?

JESSE. I already feel like I'm serving a life sentence, Miles! I'd rather do my time next to somebody who actually appreciates it!

(JESSE *exits upstairs.*)

WINNIE. Miles, who's Thomas?

MILES. I don't talk about him.

WINNIE. Then why did you say his name?

MILES. He was my son.

WINNIE. Is he still alive?

MILES. I don't know. My wife took him from me.

WINNIE. Did they drink the water?

MILES. No. By the time I figured out the secret of the spring, the years had passed for them, but not for me. She thought I was possessed. A freak.

WINNIE. I don't think you're a freak.

[MUSIC NO. 18 "TIME"]

MILES. It's time we got you home to your own family.

WINNIE. Can't I stay just a little longer?

MILES. No. If your father is anything like me, all he's doing right now is watching your front door. All he's doing is…counting the minutes.

I HAD A FARMHOUSE
WITH A GRANDFATHER CLOCK
WHERE I WOULD TEACH TIME TO MY SON
OUR LESSONS BEGAN
AT TWELVE O'CLOCK SHARP
WHEN THE HANDS WOULD COME IN AS ONE
I'D SAY, "THE BIG HAND COUNTS MINUTES,
IT'S SO TIGHTLY WOUND
IT CHASES THE SMALL HAND
TO MAKE HOURS GO ROUND"

> *(A small boy enters.* **MILES** *watches his former life play out around him.)*

I TAUGHT THOMAS
CONSTELLATIONS IN THE SKY
TO TELL A SILVER MAPLE FROM A COTTONWOOD
I TAUGHT THOMAS
TO DIVIDE AND MULTIPLY
BUT WHAT HE NEVER UNDERSTOOD WAS

TIME, AS I WATCHED HIM GROW
TIME, HE WOULD NEVER KNOW
TIME, WHERE MY REGRET RESIDES
TIME, IF I ONLY KNEW
THE WHAT AND HOW AND WHO
THAT TIME TRULY DIVIDES

> *(A woman appears and takes Thomas's hand. They exit, leaving* **MILES** *behind.)*

THERE WAS A FARMHOUSE
WITH A GRANDFATHER CLOCK
WHERE ONE DAY I WOKE UP ALONE
THEY FEARED I WAS MAGIC
THEY FEARED I WAS CURSED
BUT MOSTLY THEY FEARED THE UNKNOWN
THE BIG HAND'S THE FATHER
THE SMALL HAND'S THE SON
AND THERE NEVER CAME A TIME
WHEN THEY CAME BACK AS ONE

I TAUGHT THOMAS HOW TO CATCH A FIREFLY
HOW TO MAKE A PEBBLE SKIP AND ROWBOAT SKIM
SHE TOOK THOMAS AND NEVER SAID GOODBYE
THE ONE THING I COULD NEVER GIVE TO HIM
WAS TIME
TIME
I'M LEFT WITH NOTHING
NOTHING BUT TIME

(**WINNIE** *takes* **MILES**'s *hand.*)

WINNIE. Miles, I don't have a father anymore.

MILES. You don't?

WINNIE. No. But I'll always love him, for the rest of my life. And I promise Thomas will love you, for the rest of his.

(**MILES** *hugs* **WINNIE**. *The stage revolves.*)

Scene Four: Stump Outside Tuck Cottage

(ANGUS *finds* MAE *outside.*)

[MUSIC NO. 18A "TIME (REPRISE)"]

ANGUS. You going to be okay?

MAE. I don't know. You know what frightens me the most?

ANGUS. Another hundred years of me snoring?

MAE. No. What frightens me the most is that I'm actually a little envious of Jesse.

ANGUS. Envious?

MAE. At least he's looking forward to something again.

ANGUS. Hey. I still look forward to you.

MAE. Do you? Sometimes it's a little hard to tell, these days.

ANGUS. Of course I do. Every day. Every year.

MAE.

TIME WE'VE BEEN GRANTED SO MUCH TIME
BUT WHAT IF ALL THIS TIME
DID MORE THAN PASS US BY?
LIFE EVEN INFINITE
STILL MUST HAVE LIFE IN IT
WE KNOW IT WON'T KILL US TO TRY

(JESSE *enters the attic.*)

ANGUS.	MAE.	JESSE.	MILES.
WE'LL STAY			
MORE		WINNIE MUST	
CONNECTED		BE	
WE'LL DO	WE'LL DO	PROTECTED	
	WHAT		
WHAT WE	WE CAN	MY PARTNER	
CAN		IN CRIME	
	WE'LL STOP		
	SITTING		
WE'LL	WONDERING		
	WHY		
STOP SITTING			TIME

WONDERING WHY		THEY CAN'T MAKE ME TELL HER GOODBYE	TIME
I	I	I WON'T BE LEFT ALONE	
			I WAS LEFT ALONE
WON'T BE LEFT ALONE	WON'T BE LEFT ALONE		

ALL.

LEFT TO DROWN IN MY PRIME

LEFT WITH NOTHING

MAE.

LEFT WITH NOTHING

MILES, JESSE & ANGUS.

LEFT WITH NOTHING

> (JESSE *holds up an empty vial, pockets it, exits.*)

MILES.

NOTHING BUT

ALL.

TIME

> (*At the song's end, we are back with* **MAE** *and* **ANGUS.**)

[MUSIC NO. 18B "AFTER TIME"]

MAE. You've got to convince Winnie not to drink.

ANGUS. Aw, Mae. Can't you speak with her?

MAE. No. She needs a father – and honestly, Angus? Watching you with a real child, again, I can't think of a better father than you.

ANGUS. But I don't know the first thing about having a "talk" with a girl.

MAE. You could practice on me a little more often.

ANGUS. That's not a bad idea.

MAE. Is that a yes?

ANGUS. That's an "I love you." And a yes. I'll talk to her.

    (They embrace.)

MAE. Thank you. Her poor mother must be desperate by now.

ANGUS. Funny, I'm feeling a little "desperate" myself…

MAE. Angus Michael Tuck!

ANGUS. C'mon, dance with me!

    (We are carried on a romantic swell into:)

Scene Five: Foster Parlor

(MOTHER and NANA let the MAN IN YELLOW SUIT in.)

MAN IN YELLOW SUIT. In all my travels, I've never seen a more promising wood. It would mean a great deal to me to own it. Why, I'd treat it like my only child.

(He produces papers and a pen.)

MOTHER. Let's just get this over with.

MAN IN YELLOW SUIT. Look, I want the wood and you want the girl. It's a simple trade.

NANA. It's blackmail, is what it is.

MAN IN YELLOW SUIT. Never too old to flirt, are ya, Granny? Like my suit?

NANA. You're an evil banana.

(The MAN IN YELLOW SUIT turns to MOTHER.)

MAN IN YELLOW SUIT. Sign at the *x*. And make it legible.

(MOTHER signs, but doesn't give him the papers.)

CONSTABLE JOE. Hello? It's just Constable Joe checking in, here!

(A beat.)

HUGO. And Hugo!

MAN IN YELLOW SUIT. Send him away none the wiser, I'm warning you both. You've got more to lose than I do.

(CONSTABLE JOE and HUGO enter.)

CONSTABLE JOE. Darn it, Hugo. If you can't even open a door, how are we going to close a case?

HUGO. Excellent point, sir.

CONSTABLE JOE. Betsy, how are you?

MOTHER. I'm fine, Joe. The whole disappearance turned out to be a false alarm, is all. But thank you for checking in.

CONSTABLE JOE. So, where's our Winnie, then?

MOTHER. My friend here is going to fetch her home.

(*The* **CONSTABLE** *regards the* **MAN IN YELLOW SUIT**.)

CONSTABLE JOE. (*Coolly.*) Well, the suit I recognize – but I don't believe I got your friend's name.

MAN IN YELLOW SUIT. Don't you worry about that.

CONSTABLE JOE. Do I look worried?

HUGO. Ask about those papers.

CONSTABLE JOE. Silence, mosquito. What are those papers?

MAN IN YELLOW SUIT. Just a little business transaction.

CONSTABLE JOE. Business to do with the Fair, is it?

MAN IN YELLOW SUIT. I'm no longer affiliated with that particular operation. Which has moved on.

CONSTABLE JOE. And yet, here you are.

MAN IN YELLOW SUIT. Here I am.

HUGO. What sort of business transaction?

CONSTABLE JOE. That's right, what sort of business did you say?

MAN IN YELLOW SUIT. I didn't say.

(*A beat.*)

CONSTABLE JOE. Try.

NANA. We've sold him the wood.

CONSTABLE JOE. Really? You've sold him Treegap Wood. After all these decades. Well, neighbor, I suppose I'll be seeing you.

(**CONSTABLE JOW** *puts out his hand.* **MAN IN YELLOW SUIT** *extends his own, limply.*)

MOTHER. I apologize for wasting your time, Joe.

CONSTABLE JOE. Oh, you're never a waste of time, Betsy. Always a pleasure. Come on, Hugo.

(**CONSTABLE JOE** *and* **HUGO** *exit.*)

MAN IN YELLOW SUIT. Well done, ladies. That wasn't so hard. Now give me the contract.

MOTHER. Not until I have my daughter.

MAN IN YELLOW SUIT. Fine. I certainly don't want her.

NANA. Oh, would you drop dead, already.

MAN IN YELLOW SUIT. Never.

> *(He exits the house. The stage revolves, revealing him walking out and away from the Fosters' yard.)*

[MUSIC NO. 19 "EVERYTHING'S GOLDEN"]

JACKPOT THE FOREST IS MINE
CRACKSHOT TAKES AIM AND BULLSEYE!
MONEY ON EVERY TREE
HONEY THIS WOOD IS SOLID GOLD

Scene Six: Path Near Wood

[MUSIC NO. 20 "YOU CAN'T TRUST A MAN"]

(**MAN IN YELLOW SUIT** *dances down the road.*)

HUGO. Look at him go.

CONSTABLE JOE. Haven't seen a grown man move like that since my Uncle Pete got fire ants in his shorts.

HUGO. That sounds horrible.

CONSTABLE JOE. Oh, nooo, Hugo. It was hilarious.
(He crosses in front of **HUGO**.*)* We best be getting on.

HUGO. Would hate to let him get too far ahead.

CONSTABLE JOE. Well, a fellow dressed in yellow's not going to be hard to track.

HUGO. Sure isn't a nice yellow.

CONSTABLE JOE. Hugo, there's no such thing as a nice yellow.

HUGO. But what about…baby chickies? Or dandelions? Or corn on the cob? Or –

CONSTABLE JOE. Butter.

HUGO. Good one, sir.

CONSTABLE JOE. I don't know, Hugo. Got a bad feeling it's all going to come apart like wet bread.
YOU CAN'T TRUST A MAN DRESSED IN YELLOW
HUGO, ONLY A ROGUE WEARS THAT HUE
A MAN WHO IS FONDEST
OF SUITS THAT ARE JAUNDICED
PUTS THE YOLK ON HIM AND THE JOKE ON YOU

THEY'RE TRICKSY ALL MEN DRESSED IN YELLOW
SOMETHING DEADLY IN THEIR LIVELIHOOD
HE MUST BE COMPENSATING –

HUGO.
ALSO FABRICATING –

CONSTABLE JOE. Hugo, there you go again. Fabricating? If he hated the fabric, he would never have bought the suit!

 HE MUST BE COMPENSATING

HUGO.

 ALSO...LYING

HUGO & CONSTABLE JOE.

 'BOUT WHY HE WANTS THE FOSTERS' WOOD

CONSTABLE JOE.

 YOU CAN'T TRUST A MAN DRESSED IN YELLOW
 THAT I KNEW FROM HIS VERY FIRST HELLO
 SHOULD HAVE LOCKED HIM IN A CELL

HUGO & CONSTABLE JOE.

 OH
 YOU CAN'T TRUST A MAN

HUGO. From the carnival.

CONSTABLE JOE.

 ALSO, CARNIVAL MEN CAN'T BE TRUSTED
 SOMETHING WICKED THERE BREWS UNDERNEATH
 THOSE INBREDS REGALE YA
 WITH MAD BACCHANALIA
 THEY ALL SHARE MAYBE EIGHT TEETH

 I SAY, CARNIVAL MEN CAN'T BE TRUSTED
 FLASHY HOBOS INVADING OUR TOWNS
 THEY ASK MY PERMISSION
 TO CHARGE AN ADMISSION
 TO EXPOSE US TO CHARLATANS, ACROBATS, AND CL – CL –

HUGO. Clowns, sir?

CONSTABLE JOE. I hate them.

 A CARNIVAL MAN CAN'T BE TRUSTED
 THEY ARE ALL ACUTELY MALADJUSTED
 WHO KNOWS HOW THEIR FUNNEL CAKE IS DUSTED

HUGO & CONSTABLE JOE.

 NO YOU CAN'T TRUST A MAN –

HUGO. With a bad handshake.

CONSTABLE JOE.

DID YOU NOTICE HIS PECULIAR HANDSHAKE?

HIS FINGERS NEITHER FLACCID NOR FIRM

HUGO.

LIKE TOUCHING A PORPOISE

CONSTABLE JOE.

NO HABEAS CORPUS

COULD KEEP THAT FISH –

HUGO.

MAMMAL.

CONSTABLE JOE.

FROM SERVING FULL TERM

BAD HANDSHAKE, BAD MAN

HUGO & CONSTABLE JOE.

WATCH IT IF HIS GRIP LACKS A SQUEEZE

CONSTABLE JOE.

AND A CARNIVAL MAN CAN'T BE TRUSTED

HUGO.

AS SHIFTY AS A SWINGING TRAPEZE

HUGO & CONSTABLE JOE.

AND YOU CAN'T TRUST A MAN DRESSED IN YELLOW

EVEN IF YOU LOVE CHEDDAR CHEESE

COMINGLE ALL OF THESE

YOU'LL SEE THE RECIPE'S

ONE BAD MAN

ONE BAD MAN

ONE BAD MAN

CONSTABLE JOE. Come on, Hugo. Let's pick up the pace.

(They exit.)

Scene Seven: The Lake

[MUSIC NO. 20A "BEFORE THE WHEEL"]

(WINNIE *and* ANGUS *are in a boat on a lake.*)

WINNIE. I think I got another one!

(WINNIE *pulls in a fresh catch.*)

ANGUS. What is that: five fish in ten minutes?

WINNIE. Well, it would've been six fish, if –

ANGUS. I said I was sorry.

(*He unhooks the fish.*)

WINNIE. Did you teach Jesse and Miles to fish?

ANGUS. You bet I did.

WINNIE. What about Thomas?

ANGUS. Miles told you about Thomas? Wow.

WINNIE. Well, did you? Teach him how to fish?

ANGUS. No. Thomas was gone before I had a chance to teach him anything. Miss that boy.

WINNIE. I know what that feels like. I miss my father every day.

ANGUS. 'Course you do.

WINNIE. Mr. Angus, I had this idea.

ANGUS. O…kay.

WINNIE. If I shared the water with Mother and Nana, we'd always be there for each other.

ANGUS. Oh, sweetie. That's just not how the world's supposed to work.

[MUSIC NO. 21 "THE WHEEL"]

WINNIE. But if my father had known about the water, we would never have had to say goodbye, ever.

ANGUS. Winnie, as difficult as it is to say goodbye once, it's even harder to say it again and again. But that's just what happens when you mess with the rules of nature.

I BET YOU DIDN'T KNOW THAT THE SUN

TOOK A SHINE TO WATER
SHE DRINKS UP A BIT FLOATS IT UP TO THE SKY
WHAT SHE TAKES FROM OUR LAKE
WILL MAKE HER A STORM CLOUD
THAT RUMBLES AND TUMBLES RAIN
FROM UP HIGH, HIGH, HIGH

IT'S A WHEEL, WINNIE
THIS JOURNEY OF OURS
SUN TO LAKE TO CLOUD THAT SHOWERS
RAIN BACK TO THE LAKE BELOW
AND YOU'LL RIDE THAT WHEEL WHEREVER YOU GO

NOT A MINUTE OR MOMENT'S THE SAME
THE WHEEL, IT KEEPS YOU GUESSING
AND EVERYTHING AROUND YOU IS ALONG FOR THE RIDE
THE POND, THE BULLFROGS, THE BIRCH TREES, AND
    HOUND DOGS
PLUS PEOPLE, ALL PEOPLE EBB AND FLOW WITH THE TIDE,
    TIDE, TIDE

IT'S A WHEEL, WINNIE
A RIPPLE IN WATER
GIRL TO WIFE TO MOTHER TO DAUGHTER
LIKE ALL YOUR KINFOLK COME AND GONE
CAN'T STOP ROWING, GROWING, CHANGING, THEN MOVING
    ON

(**ANGUS** *drops an anchor. The boat stops moving.*)

ONCE YOU DROP AN ANCHOR
A BOAT GETS STUCK
AND IT COULD STAY FOREVER

WINNIE.

JUST FLOATING ON TOP

ANGUS & WINNIE.

WATCHING LIFE PASS IT BY
JUST FLOATING ON TOP

ANGUS.

SHOW ME HOW TO CLIMB BACK ON THE WHEEL
I'LL BE THERE SLICK AS A SLINGSHOT
PREPARED TO GET OFF AT THE END

AND SHARE WITH SOMEONE MY SPOT

YOU CAN'T HAVE LIVING WITHOUT DYING
SO YOU CAN'T CALL THIS LIVING WHAT WE GOT
WE JUST ARE, WE JUST BE
NO BEFORE, NO BEYOND
A ROWBOAT ANCHORED IN THE MIDDLE OF A POND

Don't be afraid of death, Winnie. Be afraid of not being truly alive. You don't need to live forever, you just need to live. Do you understand?

WINNIE. Yes.

(**WINNIE** *picks up the anchor.*)

WINNIE.	**ANGUS.**
IT'S A WHEEL	
	IT'S A WHEEL, WINNIE

ANGUS, WINNIE & ENSEMBLE.
    A RIPPLE IN WATER
    GIRL TO WIFE TO MOTHER TO DAUGHTER
    LIKE ALL YOUR KINFOLK COME AND GONE

ANGUS.	**WINNIE.**
IT'S A WHEEL, WINNIE	IT'S A WHEEL

ANGUS, WINNIE & OFFSTAGE ENSEMBLE.
    A CIRCLE IN MOTION
ANGUS & WINNIE
    CAN'T STOP ROWING, GROWING, CHANGING,
    THEN MOVING ON
    CAN'T STOP ROWING,
    GROWING,
    CHANGING
    THEN MOVING ON

(*At song's end,* **MILES** *appears at the lake's edge.*)

MILES. Pa, Hurry!

(**ANGUS** *throws a line to* **MILES** *on the dock.*)

ANGUS. What's wrong?

MILES. Jesse's gone.

[MUSIC NO. 21A "FROM BOAT TO SPRING"]

ANGUS. Jesse's always coming and going, he'll be back.

MILES. No, Pa. It's not like that this time. He didn't even say goodbye to Ma.

ANGUS. Well, that's not like him. If he hopped a train, he could be six towns out, by now.

WINNIE. He isn't on a train.

MILES. You know where he went?

WINNIE. I'm sure he's in the woods.

ANGUS. I don't like the sound of this…

MILES. Neither do I.

WINNIE. I know exactly where he is.

(**WINNIE** *leads them off.*)

Scene Eight: The Spring

[MUSIC NO. 22 "THE STORY OF THE MAN IN THE YELLOW SUIT"]

(JESSE bottles water at the spring. He backs away and pockets the vial as the MAN IN YELLOW SUIT enters.)

MAN IN YELLOW SUIT. Hold it right there, seventeen.

JESSE. You.

MAN IN YELLOW SUIT. Me! Where's your little friend? Oh, who am I foolin', I don't care – the wood is now mine.

JESSE. What?

MAN IN YELLOW SUIT. Why don't you show me what you've been hiding.

JESSE. I have no idea what you're talking about.

MAN IN YELLOW SUIT. That's simply not true.

 ONCE UPON A TIME
 ONCE UPON A TIME
 IT STARTED JUST LIKE THAT
 MY GRANNY TOLD A STORY
 HOW THAT WOMAN LOVED TO GAB

JESSE. What does this have to do with me?

MAN IN YELLOW SUIT. Only everything.

 SAID THERE WAS A MAN
 WITH A WIFE AND SONS
 AND THE STORY GOES
 THEIR BEAUTY FROZE
 SOUND LIKE ANYONE FAMILIAR
 OR SHOULD I TAKE A STAB?

JESSE. You don't know a thing about me.

MAN IN YELLOW SUIT. I know that you know where the spring is, now show it to me.

  (MILES enters, followed by MAE, ANGUS, and WINNIE.)

JESSE. Miles, it's him! This is the man!

MILES. Hold it right there!

> (As **MILES** *lifts a rifle,* **MAE** *runs to stand in front of it.*)

MAE. Miles, no. This isn't who we are. Give me the gun.

MAN IN YELLOW SUIT. My God, it's all of you. The tale comes to life, just like my granny said. I don't know why I expected something a little more…impressive.

> (**MILES** *hands* **MAE** *the rifle.*)

JESSE. But Ma, he knows the secret –

MAN IN YELLOW SUIT. – And I've been guarding it with my life!

  MY LIPS ARE SEALED
  GRANNY DIDN'T RAISE A SNITCH
  I CAN MAKE YOU FILTHY RICH
  WE'LL BOTTLE THE WATER
  SELL IT FOR A FEE
  AND SPLIT THE PROFITS EQUALLY

ANGUS. You're mad. We would never…

MAE. We just want to live our lives in peace.

MAN IN YELLOW SUIT. What is wrong with you people?

  YOU COULD BE SULTANS
  YOU COULD HAVE KINGDOMS
  YOU DIDN'T THINK OF THIS BEFORE?
  IF YOU CAN PUT ON A PRICE ON ETERNAL LIFE
  THEY'LL PAY ANYTHING AND MORE

And all you have to do is lead me to the water.

MILES. And why would we say yes?

> (*The* **MAN IN YELLOW SUIT** *pulls out a pistol.*)

MAN IN YELLOW SUIT. Here's why.

ANGUS. Your gun doesn't scare us.

MAN IN YELLOW SUIT. Of course.

> (*The* **MAN IN YELLOW SUIT** *grabs* **WINNIE,** *puts the gun to her head.*)

Now it does.

MAE. Please, no, she's just a child!

JESSE. Here. Take the water. Just let her go.

MAN IN YELLOW SUIT. My God, there it is.

    TODAY IS THE DAY

JESSE. You take this.

MAN IN YELLOW SUIT.

    THE WAITING IS OVER

JESSE. I'll show you the spring.

MAN IN YELLOW SUIT.

    THE ANSWER SO SIMPLE

    SO PERFECTLY PURE

JESSE. Please let her go.

MAN IN YELLOW SUIT.

    THE SECRET TO ETERNAL LIFE

    AND NOW I'LL NEVER –

> *(At the last moment,* **JESSE** *tosses the vial to* **MILES**.*)*

> *(The* **MAN IN YELLOW SUIT**, *furious, points his gun at* **WINNIE**.*)*

> *(***MAE** *hits him with the rifle. He crumples to the ground.)*

ANGUS. Don't look.

WINNIE. Is he…dead?

ANGUS. *(Checking the* **MAN IN YELLOW**'s *pulse)* Yes.

MAE. My God. What have I done?

ANGUS. You protected your family, is what. And nobody needs to know –

CONSTABLE JOE. *(Offstage.)* Over here, Hugo!

ANGUS. Who's that?

HUGO. *(Offstage.)* Winnie!

> *(***CONSTABLE JOE** *and* **HUGO** *run in.)*

CONSTABLE JOE. Step away from the child!

WINNIE. I'm okay, Constable Joe.

ANGUS. Winnie, you know this man?

CONSTABLE JOE. I'll be asking the questions here, starting with: *(Re: the* **MAN IN YELLOW SUIT***.)* Who's responsible for this?

WINNIE. It was m—

> *(***MAE** *steps forward, cuts* **WINNIE** *off.)*

MAE. I am, sir. And if I have to go to jail, I will.

CONSTABLE JOE. Wouldn't be jail, it'd be death by hanging.

MILES. *(Mutters.)* No, it wouldn't.

WINNIE. It's not true. I hit him. With this.

CONSTABLE JOE. You two: take this man out of the child's view.

> *(***MILES** *and* **JESSE** *take the* **MAN IN YELLOW SUIT**
> *offstage, re-enter.)*

You're safe now, Winnie. Could you tell me the real story of what's gone on here?

WINNIE. It started when that man pulled a knife on Jesse at the Fair, and then he followed us into the wood, and took out a gun, and I —

CONSTABLE JOE. *(Holding up a hand.)* On second thought, the less I know, the better. Now, give me a minute to think.

HUGO. If it was a child acting in self-defense, she'd sure get off easy…

CONSTABLE JOE. I'm thinking.

(A long beat.) I'm done. I believe you.

WINNIE. You do?

CONSTABLE JOE. Of course I do. You're Nathan Foster's daughter, aren't you?

WINNIE. Always.

CONSTABLE JOE. Now, who's the Swiss Family Robinson?

WINNIE. These are my friends.

> *(***ANGUS** *steps in.)*

ANGUS. How do. We were just passing through. Didn't mean to cause any trouble.

(They shake.)

CONSTABLE JOE. Good handshake. First thing is to reunite this girl with her poor family. Hugo, you'll take the body to town –

HUGO. Uh, Dad – I mean, Sir… I don't think I can.

CONSTABLE JOE. Okay, Hugo. You see Winnie gets back in one piece, and I'll handle the body.

HUGO. Yes, sir.

CONSTABLE JOE. You'll make deputy yet.

MAE. If there's anything we can do to help, sir…

CONSTABLE JOE. Sure is. I don't know your story but I bet it's longer than I've got time to hear. So at the risk of sounding unneighborly: how about you folks leave my town, and never turn up again.

ANGUS. You can pretend you never met us. Come on, Mae.

MAE. Wait. Winnie, I know I owe your mother an apology – but all I really want to do is congratulate her.

WINNIE. For what?

MAE. Raising you.

> *(**MAE** presses the music box into **WINNIE**'s hands.)*

Here. To remember us by.

WINNIE. I could never forget you. You just saved my life.

MAE. I think it's the other way around.

ANGUS. You reminded us that we've still got something to live for. Goodbye, Winnie.

WINNIE. Goodbye, Angus.

> *(**MAE** and **ANGUS** embrace, exit.)*

MILES. So long, kid.

> *(To **JESSE**.)* I'll wait for you up ahead.

JESSE. Really?

MILES. Really. I was hoping we could walk together.

WINNIE. *(Whispers.)* Hug him.

> *(**MILES** puts an awkward arm around **JESSE**'s shoulder, exits.)*

(JESSE turns to WINNIE, pulls out the vial, hands it to her.)

JESSE. It's all up to you now. Hide it somewhere good. Drink it when you're seventeen, and then find me. I'll leave directions somehow – and I'll be planning great adventures for us.

WINNIE. So will I.

HUGO. Ready, Winnie?

WINNIE. Ready, Hugo.

(To JESSE.*)* Think of me every time you climb a tree…
(She sticks out her hand to shake.) – or get in trouble.

(They shake.)

JESSE. Every day, then.

HUGO. Let's go.

(HUGO walks WINNIE to a clearing in the woods.)

Scene Nine: Path Back Home

[MUSIC NO. 23 "EVERLASTING"]

WINNIE.

> THERE ARE TWO WAYS HOME DOWN ONE LONG ROAD
> ONE CLEAR PATH TO TWO CONCLUSIONS
> DOES THE STORY END, OR NEVER END?
> DOES THE SECRET FADE, OR IS IT EVERLASTING?
>
> I COULD RETURN TO MY MOTHER
> LIKE NOTHING HAS HAPPENED
> LIVE LIKE AN IMPOSTER
> FOR SIX LONG YEARS
> TURN SEVENTEEN
> THEN GOOD GIRL WINNIE FOSTER
> DRINKS FROM THE VIAL
> AND HER PAST DISAPPEARS
>
> THERE ARE TWO WAYS HOME DOWN ONE LONG ROAD
> ONE CLEAR PATH TO TWO CONCLUSIONS
> DOES THE STORY END, OR NEVER END?
> DOES THE SECRET FADE, OR IS IT EVERLASTING?
>
> OR I PUT THE TUCKS BEHIND ME
> AND PULL UP THE ANCHOR
> RIDE THE WHEEL PLENTY
> FOR ALL THAT IT'S WORTH
> TURN SEVENTEEN
> THEN EIGHTEEN, THEN TWENTY
> FOR A LIFE IS THE GREATEST
> WONDER ON EARTH
>
> CAN I, SHOULD I, DO I DRINK?
> CAN I, SHOULD I, WILL I DRINK?
>
> THERE ARE TWO WAYS HOME DOWN ONE LONG ROAD
> ONE CLEAR PATH TO TWO CONCLUSIONS
> DOES THE STORY END, OR NEVER END?
> DOES THE SECRET FADE, OR IS IT EVERLASTING?
> IS IT EVERLASTING?

Scene Ten: Foster Garden

HUGO. Well, here we are. Right back where you started.

WINNIE. You know what, Hugo? It doesn't really feel like that at all.

HUGO. Just remember, Winnie: you'll always have me to protect you.

> *(We hear a croak as* **HUGO** *backs away.* **HUGO** *shrieks.)*

WINNIE. My toad!

> *(***HUGO*** recovers.)*

HUGO. Careful, toad, or a dope like me could accidentally flatten you.

WINNIE. You're not a dope, Hugo.

[MUSIC NO. 23A "WATER ON THE TOAD"]

HUGO. That's the nicest thing anyone's ever said about me.

> *(***HUGO*** exits.)*

> *(The toad croaks again.* **WINNIE** *leans down to it.)*

WINNIE. Well, I had quite an adventure, and you're to blame. I wish there were some way to thank you.

> *(The toad croaks.* **WINNIE** *gets an idea. She uncaps the vial, pours it over the toad.)*

Here. It's a dangerous world out there. Hope you're thirsty.

> *(The toad double-croaks.)*

Don't worry about me. I can always get more.

> *(He hops off.* **WINNIE** *unlatches the fence gate and runs to the front door.)*

[MUSIC NO. 24 "THE STORY OF WINNIE FOSTER"]

> *(***WINNIE*** begins dancing in her yard by herself.* **MOTHER** *and* **NANA** *come out from the house for a joyful reunion.)*

MOTHER. Winnie!

(**WINNIE** *dances around the back of the house,
the fence is struck, and she emerges as* **TEENAGE
WINNIE**. **TEENAGE WINNIE** *and* **MOTHER** *dance
playfully.*)

(**HUGO** *enters and he and* **TEENAGE WINNIE**
*dance, he courts her with flowers, she refuses,
and then accepts as* **MOTHER** *and* **NANA** *look
on.* **JESSE** *enters and watches from a distance. As*
WINNIE *and* **HUGO** *embrace, he exits.*)

(**TEENAGE WINNIE** *and* **HUGO** *disappear around
the back of the house and emerge on their wedding
day.* **MOTHER** *and* **NANA** *watch as* **CONSTABLE
JOE** *marries them –* **WINNIE** *and* **HUGO** *dance,
their family framing them in a tableau.* **NANA**
steps back; she has passed away.)

(**TEENAGE WINNIE** *dances off behind the house
and re-enters holding her infant son. As she circles
the house the son runs on, now a young boy.*
TEENAGE WINNIE *chases him; both disappear
behind the house. They emerge as* **MIDDLE-AGED
WINNIE** *and her teenage son. A teenage girl dances
on, catching his eye.* **MOTHER** *joins the tableau
as* **MIDDLE-AGED WINNIE** *and* **MIDDLE-AGED
HUGO** *watch the teenagers do the same courting
dance that they did together.* **MOTHER** *steps back;
she has passed away.*)

(*The music brightens and* **MIDDLE-AGED WINNIE**
and **MIDDLE-AGED HUGO** *are dancing at their
son's wedding – the wedding dissolves around
them and they are alone, repeating a few steps of
their courting dance. They embrace, walk around
the house, and emerge as* **OLD WINNIE** *and* **OLD
HUGO**. *They finish the courting dance, and* **OLD
HUGO** *steps back; he has passed away, leaving*
OLD WINNIE *bereft and alone.*)

(All the dancers reappear and swirl around **OLD WINNIE***. She brightens with joy as her entire life dances around her. Eleven-year-old* **WINNIE** *comes out and faces* **OLD WINNIE***. The dancers exit – the two* **WINNIES** *are alone onstage.* **WINNIE** *does a long-ago step that* **OLD WINNIE** *mirrors.* **WINNIE** *exits.* **OLD WINNIE** *takes out the music box and opens it. As the music plays, she goes into the Foster house.)*

Scene Eleven: Tucks At The Grave

(The four **TUCKS** *enter and converge at a grave.)*

MAE. "Winnie Foster Jackson. Cherished Wife. Devoted Mother. Dearest Grandmother."

ANGUS. Expert fisherman.

MILES. Looks like she led the life we never could.

MAE. May she rest in peace.

[MUSIC NO. 25 "THE WHEEL (REPRISE)"]

(The **TUCKS** *turn to leave.* **JESSE** *goes to the grave.)*

JESSE. I'll always wonder what you did with the water.

> *(As he reaches out to leave a flower, the toad from all those years ago appears from behind the headstone – and leaps into* **JESSE***'s arms.)*

MILES. You ready to keep going, Jesse? Jesse?

> *(***JESSE** *gently stuffs the toad into his satchel.)*

JESSE.
IT'S A WHEEL, WINNIE
A RIPPLE IN WATER

TUCKS.
GIRL TO WIFE TO MOTHER
   TO
DAUGHTER
LIKE ALL YOUR KINFOLK
   COME
AND GONE
CAN'T STOP ROWING,
   GROWING,
CHANGING, THEN

ENSEMBLE.
   MOVING ON   DAY NA NA DAY NA NA DAY
                              NA

MOVING ON   DAY NA DAY NA NA
MOVING ON   DAY NA NA DAY NA NA DAY
                                 NA
                             DAY NA

[MUSIC NO. 26 "BOWS"]

The End